D0952334

The
12th
Candle

Also by Kim Tomsic
The 11:11 Wish

The 12th Candle

KIM TOMSIC

KATHERINE TEGEN BOOKS
An Imprint of HarperCollins Publishers

For Steve ♥

*And for my brother John—your
kindness knew no bounds.*

Katherine Tegen Books is an imprint of HarperCollins Publishers.

The 12th Candle
Copyright © 2019 by Kim Tomsic
All rights reserved. Printed in the United States of America.
No part of this book may be used or reproduced in any manner whatsoever
without written permission except in the case of brief quotations embodied
in critical articles and reviews. For information address HarperCollins
Children's Books, a division of HarperCollins Publishers, 195 Broadway,
New York, NY 10007.
www.harpercollinschildrens.com

Library of Congress Cataloging-in-Publication Data

Names: Tomsic, Kim, author.
Title: The 12th candle / Kim Tomsic.
Other titles: Twelfth candle
Description: First edition. | New York, NY : Katherine Tegen Books, an
  imprint of HarperCollinsPublishers, [2019] | Summary: On her twelfth
  birthday, Sage wishes on a magical candle for an end to the family curse
  she believes caused many problems, including sending her father to prison.
Identifiers: LCCN 2019009718 | ISBN 9780062654977 (hardback)
Subjects: | CYAC: Blessing and cursing—Fiction. | Magic—Fiction. |
  Wishes—Fiction. | Schools—Fiction. | Prisoners' families—Fiction. |
  Birthdays—Fiction. | BISAC: JUVENILE FICTION / Fantasy & Magic. |
  JUVENILE FICTION / Social Issues / Friendship. | JUVENILE FICTION /
  Social
  Issues / Peer Pressure.
Classification: LCC PZ7.1.T626 Aah 2019 | DDC [Fic]—dc23 LC record
available at https://lccn.loc.gov/2019009718

Typography by Katie Klimowicz
19 20 21 22 23 PC/LSCH 10 9 8 7 6 5 4 3 2 1
❖
First Edition

Some people say there's no such thing as pink lightning. They also say that curses don't exist. Those people are wrong.

CHAPTER 1
DECEMBER 14

I hurry to snag the primo spot in Goldview's school cafeteria, the window seat, and I'm feeling pretty good until I notice that one table over, Priscilla is smiling at me from the second-best spot. Priscilla never smiles at me unless evil is involved.

"A little something for your buns," she says in a painfully sweet voice.

We're having hamburgers today, so she could be talking about my sesame-seed bun, but I have a rule—never trust anything said with so much sugar-lace.

Priscilla elbows Jada, and then Jada elbows Gigi. Yep, as in, Gigi who used to be *my* friend. Gigi has the decency to look down and take a bite of her burger.

Then Priscilla whispers something, and the satisfaction that spreads across her face sends a stream of dread down my back.

Still, I refuse to let Priscilla see me sweat. I pop open my orange soda and take a sip, glancing at the cafeteria line. Bailee is third from the register, so I don't have anyone to whisper with yet. If I did, I'd say there's no way I'm giving Priscilla the satisfaction of asking why she didn't take this seat or what her peppy little bun comment means. I take another fake-calm slurp of my soda and survey her lunch tray—iced tea, red apple, folded napkin, and bunless burger (Priscilla doesn't believe in eating bread). And then I notice that there on her meat patty, between the cheese and the ketchup, are two empty round spots. Her pickles are missing, and I have a good idea where they might be now.

Pasted on my behind.

Most eleven-year-olds on the verge of turning twelve would probably freak out or throw their orange soda right at Priscilla's gold headband, but that's exactly what she wants. She's like a chess player, moves planned in advance. Like two months ago, she tripped me in math class, and right when I was about to tell Mrs. Floss, Priscilla hollered, "Ouch! Mrs. Floss, Sage kicked me."

Mrs. Floss *looooves* Priscilla. Plus, my father is Carl Sassafras, and everyone knows what he's accused of, so everyone expects me to be doing something wrong, too. Needless to say, I was the one who had to apologize.

Today, instead of playing into Priscilla's sneaky plan, I make my own sugar-laced comment. "I thought today, on account of our shared birthdays, we were having a truce, but apparently, we're trading bits of our lunch. What would you like from my tray, Priscilla?"

"Huh?" she says, confused by my faux-friendly tone.

"I suppose I'll have to 'give' you something later." I put air quotes around "give" so she can get an early start on worrying about what I might do.

That drops her grin long enough for me to attempt a clean escape. I take three giant steps away from the table before she hollers at my back, "The pickles are free. No food stamps required."

She laughs all high-pitched so that the cafeteria quiets and heads turn my way.

As much as I try to squeeze my feelings behind my eyes, they still sting.

Do not, I tell myself, *do NOT let them see you tear up.*

I force myself to walk with my head held high,

one forever-long step after the next—past the sixth graders, then seventh graders, past the frozen yogurt machine and the four gold-sealed Janitor of the Year plaques hanging on the wall. Finally, I push open the cafeteria door. When it slaps shut behind me, I drop the slow-walking act and sprint to the bathroom, praying the paper towels are stocked this time.

When I arrive at the bathroom, there's a yellow handwritten sign posted on the door. It says "Eighth Grade Girls ONLY."

I don't like being bossed, but the sign makes me hesitate, which gives Bailee time to catch up, breathing hard.

"Why'd you leave when I was still in line?" she asks, fixing the crooked slant of her tortoiseshell glasses.

"Godzilla," I say, like I'm talking about armpits or toe jam. Godzilla is the perfect name for Priscilla since she's tall and likes to destroy things, and by "things" I mean me.

"I'm sorry." Bailee nods sympathetically until she notices the sign. Her words fly out in a panic. "Sage Sassafras! This bathroom is for upperclassmen, not sixth graders!"

"Not when it's an emergency." I rip the yellow paper from the door, and Bailee gasps as if I just mooned the entire art club.

"You can't go tearing down signs!"

I narrow my eyes, taking a closer look at my best friend. Sometimes she won't out-and-out say what she's worried about, but I'm an experienced guesser, especially because we've known each other since we were four. I'd bet the six dollars in my backpack Bailee is worried my sign destruction will give people another reason to accuse me of being just like my daddy.

"We'll be fine." I push open the door and go inside.

Bailee follows me, trying to grab the crumpled paper, but I toss it into the trash can. With that, her deep breathing revs, and she drums her purple-painted fingernails against her collarbone.

Shoot. I didn't mean to put Bailee in the middle of one of her worst nightmares—the one where she stresses over rules vs. germs. Now she's stuck with a choice: either snatch the sign from the garbage and face staph, *E. coli*, or whatever contagion she imagines; or leave it in the trash, *but* risk being caught alongside me—sign-destroyer/rule-breaker.

I touch her arm. "Sorry, Bay." I turn my butt toward the mirror and look over a shoulder. "Oh, sepia!" I say, because it's the crummiest color I can think of at the moment. There, on my butt, are two round pickle imprints. The actual pickles probably fell off during my jog down the hall, but the proof of their past is outlined on my white jeans.

"Oh no, Sage!" Bailee's voice fills with pity. She knows these jeans are my one new piece of school clothing, given to me by Miss Tammy, who lives next door.

I balance on my tiptoes and crane my neck for a better view. The circle marks wouldn't look so bad if the pickles had traveled straight from the jar to my behind, but these pickles came with ketchup and left a light pink outline. I sigh. "This is my own fault. I should've kept a better eye on Godzilla."

"I'm really, *really* sorry. But we should get out of here." Bailee runs her hands down her smooth dark ponytail, darting looks at the door like she's worried a SWAT team of eighth graders might come busting in. "You can borrow clothing from the office bin."

"The ugly bin?" I say. "Nooooo thank you." I reach for a paper towel, but the dispenser is empty.

"Will you please hurry?"

"Chill, Bay. Hazing's a boy thing. And what would the girls do anyhow? Make us wear ugly nail polish?" I snatch some toilet paper from the nearest stall and return to the mirror.

"A boy thing? What do you call the circles on your butt?"

"A generational feud." She knows this. I've told her

a thousand times about Momma and Mrs. Petty, who is Godzilla's momma.

"Can't you be done with that stupid feud?"

"Of course not." I wet the toilet paper. "It's a family obligation. That plus the curse doesn't leave me a choice." I rub on the pickle marks. The pink lines fade into gray circles.

"That's as good as it's going to get." Bailee turns on two faucets and flashes another worried look at the door. "Come on," she pleads. "Let's wash hands and go."

"All right already." My hands aren't dirty, but for Bailee's sake I grab a glob of soap and copy her, speed-scrubbing my palms under the warm water. I look at the mirror and besides noticing that my ponytail has frizzed and could use some fixing, I also see two flyers taped at an angle. One is white and says "Seven days until the solstice." We've already seen that flyer a thousand times today. But there's another flyer. A lavender one. "Look." I point with my chin.

The paper's edges are dotted with stars and sunbursts and the center has a drawing of a store with fancy lettering that reads "Minerva's What's-it Shoppe. Everything you could possibly wish for." I dry my hands on the sides of my pants and snatch the flyer off the mirror. "You heard of Minerva's?"

"No." Bailee shakes her hands, air-drying and waving me toward the door.

Then I notice the address. "It's at Seventh and Elm!" I say loudly. This is a big deal, because that's our side of the creek. Bear Creek divides the nice houses from the rest of us in Goldview, and there are no real stores on our side of the creek, unless you count the grocery aisle in the gas station. We just have laundromats, mechanic shops, and the Snowy Soda Brewing Factory.

"Uh-huh," Bailee says, inching me forward. "We need to g—"

The bathroom door whooshes open, my heart leapfrogs to my throat, and in walks the owner of a tight blue shirt. "What are sixth graders doing in here?"

Two friends enter behind her, and I can tell they're eighth graders on account of their boobs.

Bailee teeters on the verge of a panic attack, so I quickly crumple the lavender flyer into a ball, and in the sweetest voice possible, I say, "We've been assigned cleanup duty to keep the eighth-grade bathroom pristine." I toss it into the garbage. "That about does it, except I'll let Mrs. Downy know you're out of paper towels. I hope we've done a good job." I grab Bailee's arm. "Come on, Bay."

We hightail it out of there. But not before I hear

Blue Shirt say, "No wonder she broke into our bathroom. She's a Sassafras."

I curse my family reputation. And then I curse the curse.

CHAPTER 2

The curse followed me into life, making Priscilla and me enemies before we were even born.

We both made our appearance at Goldview County Hospital exactly twelve years ago this day, December 14, her at precisely one minute before noon and me at a minute before midnight. Momma said the nurses who oohed and ahhhed over my mop of dark hair ignored Priscilla's bald head. And the nurses who loved on Priscilla didn't pay mind to me.

But the curse dates back further than our shared birthday. It officially started when our mommas were in sixth grade right here when Goldview was a middle school and not a K-8 campus. Back then, my momma and Candice Petty, that's Priscilla's momma, were good friends. Some say they were as close as sisters, until the day they were both struck by the same bolt of pink lightning.

If you don't believe in pink lightning, let me stop you right there. Pink lightning is real, but it's rare. To see it, you need a thundersnow, which is when a snowstorm *and* a thunderstorm happen at the exact same time. People here argue about the possibility of pink lightning in Colorado because thundersnows don't happen very often. But they happen.

If you're still doubting that pink lightning is real, you can ask Steven Flores; he loves talking about weather. But if you don't trust sixth graders, then ask my science teacher. She says lightning can be different colors, depending on what the lightning flash travels through and how close it comes to the viewer. She says haze, dust, moisture, and other tiny bits in the atmosphere mess with how people see it, so lightning usually looks white or blue, but under rare circumstances like a thundersnow, the lightning appears pink.

Momma says she doesn't remember much about the day of the pink lightning except that it happened on the winter solstice. Others in town have filled in the blanks. The checkers at Sprouts confirm the lightning bolt was as pink as the cotton candy at the county fair. Mrs. Downy says it struck when Momma and Mrs. Petty were cutting across the football field, going home after track practice. And Miss Tammy, who talks to a lot of people since she works at the Goldview Café, says the power in town cut out for a full minute, and that's when Momma and Mrs. Petty were plagued with the curse—the Curse of Opposites.

Here's how the curse works: If one feels hot, the other feels cold. If one has a good hair day, the other has to make do with a hat. If one feels particularly brave, the other shakes in her boots.

Of course, some say the curse is baloney, but Mrs. Rimmels, who is my English teacher, says it is real, and Mrs. Rimmels is the smartest person in Goldview. She reads a whole book every week, never says *ain't*, and uses fancy words like *hors d'oeuvres*, which means bite-size snacks.

Furthermore, Mrs. Rimmels is an eyewitness since she's as old as a bag of dust, and I mean that in the kindest way. She's not only my English teacher, but she was also Momma and Mrs. Petty's English teacher, too, so she has seen the curse from the very beginning. Mrs. Rimmels even gave the curse its name—the Contrarium Curse. *Contrarium* is Latin for "opposite," and everyone knows all real curses have Latin names.

Here's what Mrs. Rimmels says about the curse: Back in their school days, when Momma wrote poetry, Mrs. Petty wrote prose. When Momma was dared to swim in the public pool and got the chills, Mrs. Petty broke out with a fever. And when Momma brought her pet guinea pig pup to school for show-and-tell, Mrs. Petty brought in her boa constrictor.

Naturally, after the snake mistook Momma's guinea pig for an hors d'oeuvre, the friendship took a nosedive.

Mrs. Rimmels isn't the only one who talks about the curse. Folks at the Goldview Café say that after the snake incident, the girls raced to claim the best parts of the curse first or else suffer the opposite all day long. They say Mrs. Petty made the first move and acted extra, *extra* dainty, which turned Momma into a klutz. She broke a toe before her track meet. So Momma, who is already quite pretty with her thick nut-brown hair and bright hazel eyes, fixed herself up for the barn dance. That same night, Mrs. Petty suffered a massive case of poison oak—one eye swelled shut and her cheeks broke out in red welts. And in high school, when Momma spent a year learning fortune-telling, Mrs. Petty became a Methodist.

Not everyone believes in the curse. Bailee and her family came to Goldview decades after the pink lightning incident, so they don't buy into the Contrarium Curse like townsfolk who have lived here their whole lives. Plus, Bailee only likes talking about things that bring on good luck, like finding a penny or shooting stars, but she swears curses are mind over matter. And since she wants to be a lawyer one day, she can't focus on negative mojo. She says that might mess her up during a trial.

I try to tell her the Contrarium Curse is why I have a gap between my front teeth and Priscilla's teeth crowd in her mouth. It's why I can smooth-whisper nice and quiet and Priscilla sandpaper-whispers all loud and harsh. It's why I'm good at reading and Priscilla is good at math. Bailee laughs at this. She and her momma call the curse nonsense, and I'm not going to lie—their skepticism is kind of nice. I like hearing them say a person gets to choose their own path. They claim that I'm not tied to the curse *or* my daddy's reputation.

I wish that were true.

CHAPTER 3

Before lunch ends, Bailee and I each grab a cone of tart frozen yogurt. It comes free with lunch, and thank goodness, because I'm starving from skipping my burger. We lick our yogurts and head around the side of the school toward our "specials" class in the library with Mr. Lehman. Under normal circumstances, I might feel miserable after dealing with Priscilla's pickle attack, but Friday's special is my favorite—art.

Outside the library door, Bailee swallows the last bite of her cone, probably because of the no-food rule and her loving the law. I take my time and say, "Save us the table on the left."

"I know," she says. "Best natural light."

Bailee goes through the nonfiction section, and I weave through the shelves of picture books and then through the novels, not only so I can finish the yogurt, but also to see what Mr. Lehman has on his display tower. This week's tower has books about some kind of weather marvel. I pop the final bite of cone into my mouth and reach for a book with lightning on the cover.

"Sage," I hear from behind me.

I turn.

"You're not about to pick up that book with sticky yogurt hands, are you?" Mr. Lehman says, lifting a bushy eyebrow above the rim of his glasses.

"Sorry." I lick my fingers and drop my arms to my sides.

"Happy birthday," he says sternly, but his eyes crinkle into a smile. Then he looks at his watch. "It's time."

We hurry down aisles of tall bookshelves toward the open space with the round tables. Aside from the gym, the library is the biggest room in our school. Once you're seated at any one of the round tables, you can see the tree-lined mountains that surround Gold-view.

We come out at the end of the aisle and just like

every day, my breath catches. The mountains are beautiful. If this were a normal December, the mountains would be covered in fluffy white snow. This year it's weird, though. There's not a single snowflake. Instead, full leafy trees hold on to every shade of fall, and the mountainside bursts with color.

"Another gorgeous autumn day," Mr. Lehman says. "You think winter weather will come this year?"

I like how he wants to know my opinion, so I think for a moment. "I kind of wish it would stay like this a while longer. That way we can have extra time living in color before everything turns white." Art teachers appreciate knowing when you think about stuff like that.

"That's a nice wish." He continues staring out the window. "It just might come true. Some consider Goldview's strange weather to be magical."

I smile, but I'm thinking if wishes were real, my daddy would still be around.

"Go on now. Have a seat."

I take a few steps forward and nearly trip when I notice who's at my table—Hudson, Steven, and Bailee are faces I expect to see, but Priscilla and Jada are there, too. Everyone's talking and acting like it's no big deal when it *is* a big deal. Hudson and Steven don't choose anyone's side in the feud—they are my friends *and* Priscilla's friends. But I expect Priscilla to choose a side, as in, a side of the room where I am not going to sit.

I know why she's cozied up in my zone, though. She's currently crushing on Steven. I sigh. Sure, he's interesting—he knows a ton about weather, his grandparents live in Honduras, and he has flown on an airplane three times. He's also cute—he's the only kid in sixth grade who doesn't get pimples, and his glossy black hair is cut in the latest boy-band fashion—but seriously, it's ridiculous that Priscilla will do anything for his attention, including sit where she's not wanted.

Bailee gives me a what-do-we-do shrug.

"Go on," Mr. Lehman says.

Instead of sulking toward them, I decide on a good attitude. Like I said—it's Friday and art class, after all.

"Hey, guys." I smile at Hudson and Steven.

"Hey," they say. Steven peels off his hoodie. Underneath, he's wearing his latest weather T-shirt. It says "What the hail."

I pull out my chair and inspect it for booby traps. Once I see it's all clear, I sit and check out the table, and now my smile stretches wide. Every student's spot has a big white sheet of paper in front of it, and I'm not talking regular paper, but the heavy kind with texture.

"Whoa," I say, feeling the paper's grain.

"I know," Hudson says. "Mr. Lehman's letting us use the acrylic paints, too."

In the center of each table sits a jar full of brushes, and next to that a bunch of tubes of paint. If a heart can glow and dance and sing, that's what mine is doing right now. Hudson's, too. We thumb through the colors—alizarin crimson, cadmium orange, burnt sienna, Hooker's green, cobalt blue, dioxazine purple.

"Okay, people," Mr. Lehman says, forcing my attention away from the paints. "It's time for the Friday Flores Report." He turns to Steven. "We're ready for your weather forecast, Mr. Flores."

"*Gracias,* Mr. Lehman." Steven stands and fakes like his thumb is a microphone. "Coming to you live from Goldview's scenic library, this is the Flores Phenom here to report," he glances out the window, "another week of autumn."

Half the students groan.

"Ugh," Priscilla says. "I'm ready for ski season."

"And snowball fights," Hudson says.

"And holiday decorations," Jada says. "Mr. Lehman, could we at least put up a menorah and Christmas tree in the library?"

"I'm sorry, as a member of the city council, I stand by our decision. No holiday decorations in town until the last leaf falls."

"Why?" Steven says.

"It's been that way for decades."

"Yeah, but why?" Steven repeats.

"Ahhh, good question." Mr. Lehman clears his throat. "Goldview doesn't want to hurry in the holidays. In other towns, when Halloween ends, people rush to plaster up winter decorations without pausing for Thanksgiving. That's why our town's culture is focused on a longer season of gratitude. Some suspect all the goodwill and gratitude is why Goldview's weather is so enchanted." He winks at us. "To accomplish a longer season of thanksgiving, we decided not to allow any winter or holiday decorations until the final leaf falls."

More groans.

"Okay, people, moving on. Before we begin our project, which I am calling 'The Forever Fall,'" he pauses and waves his arms toward the windows, "stop and appreciate the view. Rather than seeing everything, choose a focal point to paint. Also, I'd like to go over the rules of using paint in the library. First rule, there's no walking from table to table. Second rule—"

I tune out and gaze toward the window again. The sun shines on ten thousand vibrant and competing colors. A breeze makes the leaves dance. They sway, but not one comes loose. On the far left, I notice a copse of aspen trees with stark white bark and pear-yellow leaves. That's what I'll paint.

"Excuse me, Mr. Lehman," Steven says. "Can we paint a tall staircase and do a different kind of forever fall?"

Priscilla giggles in such an annoying way that I forget my happy attitude for a second and roll my eyes.

"It's your project to create as you choose," Mr. Lehman says.

Steven picks up a brush.

"Hold on a moment." Mr. Lehman takes his phone from his pocket and clicks some buttons. "Yes, here it is. Before we begin, I have a special announcement." He pushes his glasses up his nose. "There is a company called Noodler, located right in Denver." The way he says "Noodler" it's like we've never used the internet. Noodler is only the biggest search engine company in the world.

"They sent a notice announcing they're sponsoring a nationwide contest, and they've selected our school and five others around the Denver metro area to compete for a chance to represent Colorado. We hope to see a Goldview K–8 student come out on top."

Jada crosses her fingers and whispers, "I hope it's an acting competition."

Priscilla shoots her hand in the air. "Is it a math contest? You know I'm the best mathematician in Goldview."

Mr. Lehman smiles even though Priscilla is super-irritating. "It's not a math contest," he says, "but it's just as good. Several of you excel in the arts. Doodle for Noodler is a contest with a prize for the most creative artist."

I sit up. I'm pretty certain he's talking to me, because I am Goldview K–8's best artist. Well, Hudson and I are.

Hudson shoots his hand in the air and waits to be called on, because he has manners.

"Yes, Hudson."

"What's the prize?"

"Great question." Mr. Lehman adjusts his glasses. "I'll tell you about the contest first, and then we'll discuss the riches."

"Riches! Alrighty!" I clap my hands. "What is Doodle for Noodler?" Oh, shoot, I forgot to raise my hand.

Mr. Lehman doesn't get mad. His eyes do their extra-crinkly smile thingy. "Noodler challenges students to artistically draw the Noodler logo in a way that represents a theme. For example, one year the theme was 'Coming Home' and the winner drew a girl running to the arms of a father who was returning from war."

"Huh," Steven says. "Do you have another example?"

"Sure." Mr. Lehman clicks some buttons on his phone. "Another year, the theme was 'If I Could Travel In Time.' A sixth-grade winner drew futuristic buildings that formed the Noodler logo."

"Mr. Lehman," I say, "what's this year's—"

"Ah-hem." Priscilla fake-clears her throat and sandpaper-whispers, "You weren't called on, Weed."

I roll my eyes. Godzilla calls me Weed regularly, thinking it's *sooooooooo* clever, since sage grows in a garden and weeds grow in a garden. "Neither were you, Godzilla."

"Girls," Mr. Lehman says.

"Sorry." I swallow. "What is Noodler's theme this year?"

"This year's theme is 'Family.'"

Excited chatter breaks out.

Bailee nudges me. "I bet you win this, Sage."

"Should be easy for you to draw," Godzilla whispers. "All you have to do is sketch a set of prison bars."

Her words kick me in the stomach.

Jada elbows Priscilla. I think it's to egg her on, but she whispers, "Can't you call a truce on your shared birthday?"

At least nobody else at my table is watching Priscilla dad-shame me. Hudson is listening to Mr. Lehman and holding his hand in the air.

"You must maintain a B average," Mr. Lehman says, "and be in good standing with Goldview K–8 to participate. That means good grades and no detentions." He looks at Hudson's raised hand. "Yes, Hudson. What's your question?"

"Sorry to ask again, but what about the reward? What's the prize?"

A hush falls over the classroom.

Mr. Lehman smiles big-time. "The winner will receive a ten-thousand-dollar college scholarship, be interviewed by the local press and possibly national news outlets, receive tickets to the Mimi Glosser concert, and have their art displayed on Noodler's worldwide homepage for a full week."

Priscilla slaps a hand to her heart. "I could be famous!"

I snort.

"What?" Priscilla snaps at me.

"You're not even the third- or fourth-best artist in our school," I say.

"*Somebody* will be famous," Steven says.

And then it hits me. Famous.

FAMOUS!

The word sinks into my brain and grows and doubles.

Suddenly, I'm holding my breath, because I don't want anyone to see how badly I want this. Sure, a ten-thousand-dollar scholarship would be nice, but more important, I could be famous instead of infamous!

I could change my reputation in Goldview, and not be known just because everyone believes my daddy is bad. If I win, my reputation would be all my own—World-Famous Artist! Me winning could alter the reputation of the Sassafras family and finally make my life perfect!

CHAPTER 4

Bailee and I walk to English class, me tugging down my purple T-shirt to hide my pickle-stained butt and whispering about my fame theory. When we arrive at room 12, it smells like a sugar-sweet bakery—*mmm-mm*. Sitting on Mrs. Rimmels's desk is the Friday donut.

I smile at my favorite teacher.

Her hair is in a soft gray bun and she's wearing a bright floral dress with side pockets for the Kleenex she carries. She's also wearing a "Be Kind" button pinned to her crocheted collar. "Happy birthday, Miss Sage Sassafras."

Her words feel like a hug, and I give her my warmest

smile. "Thank you."

Bailee and I head to our seats, me eyeballing that donut.

Mrs. Rimmels's homemade donuts are legendary—delicious pillows of sweetened bread covered in a glaze of sugar crystals, *and* as if that's not enough, the insides are filled with creamy milk chocolate. *Mmmmm.*

Every Thursday night, Mrs. Rimmels makes her donuts, and then on Fridays, she brings them to school. She gives one to the principal; one to the school secretary; one to the school nurse; one to Mrs. Downy, who is Goldview's janitor; one to Mr. Melvin, our bus driver; and one to each teacher, which leaves the one on her desk. Mrs. Rimmels saves that donut as the prize for the student who contributed the most to the week's classroom discussion.

Sometimes my stomach growls loud enough to be heard across state borders. Today's growl probably reaches California.

Bailee leans toward me. "Holy magenta, Sage. Is that you?"

"Yep." I take a sip from my water bottle. "And that better be my donut." I don't say this because I'm hungry or braggy, but because I deserve it. I'm pretty sure I aced the quiz we took yesterday, and bigger than that, Mrs. Rimmels *loooooved* what I said about

The Outsiders. That's the novel our class is reading. I compared the book's main character, Ponyboy, to the character Aladdin and said they are both judged like they're bad people and nothing more than street rats. But it turns out they're good and smart and way more than their circumstances.

"I hope you win," Bailee says, snagging a Clorox wipe from her backpack and scrubbing down her desktop with it. She takes out her composition notebook, *The Outsiders,* and a blue pen. I imagine this will be how she'll set up in court one day, minus the novel.

Mrs. Rimmels greets more students. I open my notebook and doodle the Noodler logo. I put a party hat on the *N* and then I'm drawing each *O* into a five-layer cake when Godzilla walks in.

"Listen," I say to Bailee, nodding toward my swamp-green enemy.

Sure enough, Mrs. Rimmels says, "Happy birthday, Miss Priscilla Petty."

"See," I whisper.

Bailee scrunches her eyebrows.

"Come on. It's so obvious the way Mrs. Rimmels said 'Priscilla,' it's like she's talking about cornmeal or cement. When she said my name, it was all Cocoa Puffs and Jacuzzi-sounding. You heard it, right?"

"Yep." Bailee bites her lower lip. She always bites

her lower lip when she fibs, but I smile anyhow.

Students continue filing in, and I add frosting to my doodle.

"I'll bet you read a whole chapter ahead," Bay says, opening her book.

"Well, yeah." I say this cocky, but in a way that she knows I'm kidding. I don't tell her I actually finished the book, because that would be real bragging.

Priscilla fluffs her hair. She's still talking and hogging Mrs. Rimmels like she's the only one who matters. "Do you like my new headband?"

Ugh. Her voice grates on my nerves.

Mrs. Rimmels gives a nod. "It's very pretty."

I'd never admit it out loud, but the gold headband is pretty and looks nice with Priscilla's blond hair.

"It was the first gift I opened today." Priscilla is practically shouting even though she's standing close enough for Mrs. Rimmels's hearing aids to work. "Given to me at my birthday breakfast. Mother and Daddy had it sitting right next to my yogurt parfait, along with a pair of tickets to the Mimi Glosser concert at the Pepsi Center in January."

I don't usually let jealousy slip in, but its green slime creeps up on me now, not because of the concert or the headband, but because she got to have breakfast with her mom and dad. My daddy, well . . . he's not home. And my momma had to go in early for her job at the Snowy Soda factory like she does every morning, plus tonight, she'll come home late.

At least Momma remembered it was my birthday. She left a note for me on the back of a past-due Xcel Energy bill that said "Happy birthday, Sage!" She drew pink hearts around my name and also wrote, "I can't skip class after work tonight since I have a test, but we'll celebrate as soon as I get home. Please pick up a cake mix after school. Any kind you'd like!" Beside the note sat a tower of quarters, which means the cake mix is coming out of our laundromat budget.

Godzilla is still yammering at Mrs. Rimmels, saying something about her fancy new sandals.

I look down. The sandals are strappy and tan and she can still wear them with this oddly warm weather, and . . . and . . . huh? Something on the mushroom-gray carpet moves by Priscilla's pink-painted toes.

I lean forward and can't believe my eyes. It's a cricket! Right by her foot! It's like the universe and the curse are suddenly on my side—everyone knows Priscilla hates crickets!

". . . plus I'll open my real gifts at my party this weekend," she says.

Jada sees the cricket, too. She touches Priscilla's arm.

Here goes! I sit up, waiting to see Priscilla lose it over a little bug. Waiting to see her embarrass herself and then feel stupid. If I had a cell phone, I'd record this. Maybe somebody will record it! And post it! And it'll go viral!

"Um." Jada can't seem to think of how to tell her, and settles on pointing.

"Huh?" Priscilla says, until, "Ohh!" Her voice rings high and she hops back. "OH!" She clutches Jada's arm and panic rises in her face.

Yes! Let's get this karma-show on the road!

But before the full freak out has a chance to unfold, Ryan scoops up the cricket in his bare hands and cups them closed.

"Okay if I run this outside?" he asks Mrs. Rimmels.

"Thank you, Ryan. Wash your hands before you come back."

And that's it. Priscilla takes a breath and picks up blabbering where she left off.

The bell rings, and Mrs. Rimmels continues listening to Priscilla's nonstop chatter.

I sigh and return to doodling. My Noodler birthday sketch is coming out pretty decent. I work my pencil to turn the *L* into a candle and think how Priscilla probably has twelve candles at her house. At my apartment, there are stubs of candles—four blue, three purple, and four yellow. I don't mind that they are pre-used and short, or that they still have bits of hardened cake on the bottom. But there are only eleven. Anyone knows you can't turn twelve with just eleven candles. It makes me wonder if Minerva's What's-it Shoppe sells candles on the cheap.

In the Contrarium Curse, Priscilla inherited the responsible momma who has pockets of money and probably never forgets to buy birthday candles or groceries. At least my momma got kindness in the exchange. Babies stop crying when my momma holds them, and lost dogs run to her when she whistles. Lost dogs look at Priscilla Petty's momma like she's the dog catcher. My momma would've carried that cricket outside, too. I can guarantee you Mrs. Petty is a bug stomper.

I try to interrupt. "We're having German chocolate cake for my birthday." Priscilla doesn't zip it, so I make my voice louder. "With Cherry Garcia ice cream." My eye twitches because the Cherry Garcia part is a lie. Six dollars won't buy a cake mix, candles, *and* ice cream.

"That sounds lovely," Mrs. Rimmels says, and I can tell she means it.

Ryan returns to the room. Mrs. Rimmels smiles at him and says, "Great. Everyone is here. Now please take a seat."

"And this weekend," I say, "Bailee and I are going to see *Star Wars*."

Priscilla looks over a shoulder on the way to her desk. "You have tickets to opening day of the newest *Star Wars* movie in Denver?" Her tone accuses me of being the world's biggest liar.

"Nope." I cross my arms over my chest. "To the original *Star Wars*." I love the original *Star Wars* trilogy, because—spoiler alert—in *The Empire Strikes Back*, we find out Darth Vader is Luke's father, but everyone can see Luke is a good guy no matter what his daddy did.

"Ewwww, at the dollar theater?" Priscilla says in a low voice so Mrs. Rimmels's hearing aids won't pick up her meanness—she's good at hiding her scaly side in front of teachers. "All the cockroaches there should make you feel right at home, Weed."

"You're such a jerk, Godzilla."

"Better than a thief, Weed."

The skin on my neck warms.

". . . goes to Sage," Mrs. Rimmels says.

I'm between fuming and wanting to cry.

"Sage," Bailee whispers, "Mrs. Rimmels just said you won the Friday donut."

Mrs. Rimmels is smiling at me. At least I'm still her favorite.

I stand up and walk to her desk. "Thank you, Mrs. Rimmels."

She pulls a Kleenex from her pocket and slips it to me. "Good job, Sage. You earned the highest grade on yesterday's quiz. A ninety-seven."

Like I said, in the Contrarium Curse, my family won in the reading department whereas Priscilla was gifted with math. Bailee claims it doesn't have to be one or the other, but like I also said, Bailee doesn't understand the curse.

"Would you mind handing back the quizzes before taking your donut?" Mrs. Rimmels asks.

I happily agree and pass out the papers. I won't mention Priscilla's test grade because of confidentiality and because paper passer is a highly trusted role, but let's just say Priscilla's grade starts with the second letter of the alphabet and has a minus sign after it.

"And Priscilla," Mrs. Rimmels says, "would you like to hand out the permission forms for the winter solstice dance?"

Excited chatter buzzes through the room. The winter solstice is a big deal at our school. Classes are canceled and we celebrate with a sunset dance. The Lab Rats, aka the science club, have been hanging countdown posters every day since December 1. They'll keep hanging posters until the solstice on December 21, which is next Friday, one week from today.

"Remember," Mrs. Rimmels says, "we celebrate as a school. This is not a matchmaking service, so girls and boys, please don't worry about asking each other on a date. Just come and have a good time."

Priscilla takes the pile from Mrs. Rimmels, and now we're both paper passers, which would make this a great opportunity to sneak the chocolate donut onto her seat. But I'm not dumb. There's no way I'm risking my standing as favorite student or wasting a perfectly good donut. I'll think up a better idea later.

"The dance is just seven days away," Mrs. Rimmels says. "Please ask your parents to come as chaperones. We still need volunteers."

I pick up my donut, tear it in half, and give the other half to Bailee. When I return to my seat, I notice Priscilla has placed a form on everyone's desktop except mine, the jerk, so I snatch the one from her spot.

"Oh, right. It's a free dance," Priscilla says. "Even the street rats are allowed."

I ball my hands into fists and wish I could punch Godzilla right in that smug face. I may not think of my revenge today, but I will get her.

CHAPTER 5

I climb on the bus and plop my backpack on the seat next to me to save it for Bailee. We always choose the same spot, nine rows down on the right, me by the window, her by the aisle. Ours is one of the few seats without rips in the vinyl.

Hudson comes down the aisle after me.

"Hey, Hud."

"Hey, Sage." He drops onto the bench next to Steven and across from me.

Steven waves a book titled *Fact or Fiction Weather Marvels*. "Listen to this," he says. "Goldview has more weather marvels than anywhere else in the world, but Salt Lake City, Utah, and Bozeman, Montana, have around six thundersnows a year, and so do Nova Scotia, Amman, and Jerusalem."

"For real?" I say. "They have pink lightning, too?"

Steven nods and keeps reading.

Ryan scoots into the row behind Hudson and Steven. He smooths down his green Lab Rats T-shirt. "You guys are coming to the solstice dance, right?"

"Wouldn't miss it," I say.

"Yep," Hudson and Steven say at the same time.

"Yo, Sage." Hudson turns to me and wags his eyebrows. "Better watch out for me in the Noodler contest. I might win this time."

"You might," I say. And he could.

Hudson and I have a long-running art rivalry. In kindergarten, we'd compare the stickers the teacher put on our drawings, trying to decode whose art piece she thought was better. Last year, Sprouts had a "draw the bag" contest for kids to design the store's new canvas grocery sacks. They said each artist could turn in anything he or she wanted.

I loved hearing them call us artists, something Daddy used to call me when he lived at home.

Anyhow, I won, but Hudson was a close second. Sprouts gave both of us a gift card and a free bag each.

"Good luck," I tell Hudson, and mean it, even though he's my toughest competition and my future reputation is on the line.

"Don't worry about giving Hudson luck," Steve says. *"Mi hermano tiene mucho talento."*

"Okay?" I say, laughing. "I understood the 'talent' part."

"All you need to know is that my bro is the OG," Steven says.

Hudson laughs and Ryan says, "Yep," and pats Hudson on the back, which quickly turns into wrestling and nearly knocks off Hudson's baseball cap. He turns his cap backward, his wheat-colored hair curling out the bottom. "Okay, everyone careful now. I'm taking out the XJZ2000."

The XJZ2000 is Hudson's fancy phone. Even though his mom buys the on-sale apples from the same bin as my momma, he has a phone because his grandparents gave it to him so they can call him anytime they want.

Ryan leans over Hudson's shoulder and says, "Are you checking if Fortnite announced their new release date?"

"Nah. I'm looking up past Noodler winners."

Hudson types on his phone, and more kids climb on the bus and fill up seats. And then Godzilla struts down the aisle!

Mustard yellow, I think, because I always think in ugly colors when I'm facing a lousy situation.

Priscilla never rides the bus, and I am not prepared

to deal with her again today. I have a theory that I only have one hundred Priscilla energy units per day, and according to my theory I've used them all up. To make matters worse, she plops down in the seat right in front of me. This is normally Curtis's seat, and I like Curtis. He tells Bailee and me funny jokes and never says anything about my daddy.

Priscilla fluffs her hair and turns sideways, giving me another close-up of her fancy headband. Jada sits next to Priscilla.

I turn to my window and scan the parking lot, wondering why Mrs. Petty isn't here for her. Priscilla's momma always picks her up in their fancy black Tesla, honking the horn in case everyone isn't already looking at her shiny car.

"Hi, guys," Priscilla says, all bubbles and smiles. "Hey, Steven. You killed it with the Flores Report today."

Ohhhh. Steven. Right. That's why she's here.

She hands each of the boys a bright blue envelope that's been sealed with a gold sticker and says, "You are cordially invited to my birthday party tomorrow."

Hudson, still busy with his phone, says, "Thanks." He slides the envelope under his leg and says, "Whoa, Sage. Check out this eighth grader in Ohio who won the contest last year! His art is really good."

He flashes his phone screen my way. "Says here he used Inkscape to make the color pop like that."

I try to keep my face neutral so he doesn't clue in that I have no idea what he's talking about. "Hmmm."

Priscilla spins around, her vinyl seat crunching. "You know about Inkscape?"

"Sure." My eye twitches.

"You're not actually thinking of entering the contest, are you?" The fake sweetness vibrates in Godzilla's cruel voice.

My chest tightens. I buy a second with a shoulder shrug.

"Of course she is going to enter," Hudson says. "Why wouldn't she?"

Have I mentioned Hudson is a good friend?

Priscilla presses her lips closed and raises her eyebrows like she's trying not to spill a big funny secret. I know she's trying to make me feel puny. Too bad it works.

Gigi comes down the bus aisle and pauses for a moment when she sees Priscilla and Jada. Then she rearranges her face. "Hey?" She says it to Jada and Priscilla before taking the seat in front of them. Priscilla leans forward and whispers something to Gigi. Gigi laughs all low and with short bursts. It's not her real laugh. I remember her real laugh was high and stretched out.

Back in fifth grade, Gigi used to sit next to Bailee and me. I'd sit by the window, Gigi in the middle, and Bailee on the outside. The three of us loved it. We'd squeeze in and I'd duck so Mr. Melvin, the bus driver, wouldn't know there were three in a seat. Nowadays, she sits several rows in front of us and barely says hello.

Curtis gets on the bus next and sits in the row behind me, since Priscilla stole his seat. And here's the thing: He doesn't grumble or anything. Instead, he smiles like the more the merrier. Curtis is easygoing like that.

Priscilla reaches past me and hands an envelope to Curtis before she giggles at me again.

"What did I miss? What's so funny?" Ryan asks.

Priscilla tosses her hair. "Well, you guys know this," she says to the boys. She turns to me. "But you may not, Sage." She clears her throat and speaks slowly like I'm in preschool. "Noodler is a technology giant."

"Duh," I say, because everyone knows that's always a good comeback.

"Do you even own a laptop?"

The puny feeling spreads through my stomach. "Of course I do."

Gigi darts a look over her shoulder but doesn't call out my lie.

"That's a start. How about a tablet and pencil stylus

or a subscription to the Adobe Creative Cloud?" Priscilla says. "All good artists use Illustrator, you know."

Hudson is nodding, saying yes for me, expecting or maybe hoping I have one of those things. But I don't. Maybe I don't have what it takes to participate in a contest for a tech giant.

Priscilla turns to Jada. "She's either a thief or a liar." She makes sure to say this loud enough for the whole bus to hear.

I stare out the window at the tops of heads making their way down the sidewalk. I wish I lived close enough to get off the bus and walk home.

"Don't, Priscilla," Jada whispers.

Priscilla *tsks*. "What? I'm just saying it feels suspicious if she really has Creative Cloud. It costs over fifty dollars. My cousin told me so, and she's a real artist."

The news about what I don't have for the competition piles on my chest, brick by brick. Fifty dollars is an impossible number.

"Per month," Ryan says. "My dad subscribes." He doesn't say this in a snotty way, but more factually.

"She doesn't need Illustrator," Hudson says. "Procreate is a great program, and so much cheaper."

I stay still, trying to keep the worry from choking my heart. How come I don't know about these art programs?

They continue talking about technology I'll never be able to afford and using words I've never heard like Wacom and Creative Cloud and iPencil. Okay, I've heard of an eye pencil, but the only one I've ever seen is the blue kind Miss Tammy uses too much of before her shift at the café.

Suddenly, Bailee plops down next to me. "Hey?" She hesitates before whispering, "What in the mustard yellow is going on?" I taught her the color thing.

My struggle to spit out a quick answer is enough for Godzilla to realize she has successfully unnerved me. She seizes the moment and blasts her best condescending voice. "It's common sense, Sassafras. You can't go entering a technology giant's art contest without using technology. You know Noodler is not looking for a crayon drawing, right?"

The flush burns across my face, and I manage a shrug that comes out as an awkward twitch.

Bailee squeezes hand sanitizer from the keychain looped on the end of her backpack. She rubs her palms, waiting for me to defend myself as I usually do, but when I stay silent, she says, "Sage could draw with a piece of bark in the dirt and it'd still be the best thing anyone has ever seen."

"True that," Hudson says.

My insides lift to a little less slouchy.

Priscilla rolls her eyes. "Whatever. I'm just saying this isn't a Sprouts Farmers Market grocery store contest. This is Noodler. I mean, geez, you understand that, right? Noodler!" Then she says, "They probably do background checks. I don't think they'd like a convicted felon in their contest. It ruins their brand and all, you know?"

I want to snap some witty comment back, but so much shame has slipped under my skin that my mouth dries.

"Sage isn't a felon," Bailee says.

Priscilla seizes this moment to spit out the words she knows will hurt me the most. "Well, her father is."

CHAPTER 6

"All aboard?" Mr. Melvin counts the number of elementary kids up front and us in the back.

"Yep!" someone shouts.

"Alrighty." Mr. Melvin cranks the door closed and turns on what he calls his Funky Friday Tunes, and we start moving.

"You okay?" Bailee whispers.

I sit perfectly still and make a small sound, enough for Bailee to know I don't want to talk in front of everyone.

Bailee gives my arm a we'll-talk-later squeeze and turns around to listen to Curtis tell jokes. Hudson messes with his phone, and Steven and Ryan talk basketball. Priscilla noses in on the basketball conversation, not only to impress Steven, but also because in the Contrarium, she took the sporty skills.

My cheeks sting and my ears buzz. I stare out the window at passing cars and gold, leafy trees. Godzilla continues yapping, and now she's loud-whispering to someone about her felon comment, because she likes to remind everyone that her daddy is president of Goldview First National Bank, whereas my daddy was convicted of trying to rob that same bank.

Godzilla sucks.

Nobody on the bus with two ears is surprised by the bank news. My daddy's conviction is already a month old, plus Goldview is small and people like to talk.

But Priscilla bringing it up mortifies me all over again. I have to remind myself about the Noodler contest, and how I'll go from infamous to famous. *Infamous to famous.* It keeps me from crying.

I wish I could tell everyone that the jury got it wrong. My daddy didn't do it. He couldn't have. He wouldn't do that to me and Momma. But I don't say anything, because if I move a muscle, I might crumble.

It wouldn't matter anyhow, because no matter what I say, it doesn't stop the gossips in town. For the record, it's a lie when people say my daddy carried a gun. He's never owned a gun. It's a lie when they say he tried to break in at night and was caught because of a silent alarm, when the truth is, he was at the wrong place at the wrong time, and that could happen to anybody. The gossips even claim Momma and I were with him. I've never been to the bank at night, so that just shows how wrong they are.

Godzilla is the worst gossip of all. It's like she's on a mission to convince everyone I'm a thief "just like my daddy," and so kids in my class keep a close eye on their lunch money. Now she's poisoning the bus crowd, too.

I wish everyone could know my daddy is a whole lot more than what he's accused of. He's the one who read all the Harry Potter books with me, who took me yard sale shopping on Saturdays, who made my breakfast every morning—fancy things like frittatas and cinnamon French toast. Daddy is who I could talk to when things were rough, like when Ryan threw a snowball in my face when we were in fourth grade, and the snowball was icy and scraped my cheek, and I cried. Naturally, we didn't tell Momma because Ryan didn't mean to hurt me, and Momma would've made a stink.

Daddy is the one who I could tell my secrets to—things Momma wouldn't understand. Now that he's in prison, I keep secrets inside. And nobody cooks breakfast. Today, all I ate was the powdery bottom of an empty cereal box, because Momma forgot to buy groceries. Again.

I sniffle. The bus picks up speed.

"Sage?" Bailee whispers.

"Not now." I squeeze my insides, trying to push down the welling emotions. Red and gold leaves flash by the window, and a new lump grows in my throat. This will be the first birthday my daddy misses. When he was home, he'd paint a special birthday card for me with watercolors. He was really good at painting, but he'd say I was the best artist in the house, possibly the best in town!

He loved to hang up my drawings. By the time I was in third grade, Daddy had plastered my art over every inch of the refrigerator. Momma laughed and said, "Carl. You have to pick your favorites."

That's when Daddy and I started visiting the Saturday-morning yard sales, hunting for frames. He didn't care if a frame already had something in it. He'd lay my picture right on top of the old painting and tell me I was good enough to have my art in the Louvre, which is a famous museum in France. I didn't care if what he said was true or not; he loved my pictures and he loved me.

The bus bumps over the railroad tracks and wobbles me back to the present, Priscilla still yakking, Bailee now reading and turning a page in her book, Jada fluffing her 'fro. I twirl the end of my ponytail, staring out the window as we pass McGuckins Hardware Store. Daddy and I bought nails there, and he hammered them all over the walls at our house so he could line my framed pictures up and down our hallway.

We had a hallway and a house once. But after Daddy came home on bail, we had to move into the apartment. There were too many lawyer bills and not enough money to pay for a house anymore.

The lump in my throat doubles in size. If I don't stop thinking about my daddy, I'll either get teary-eyed and people will think I'm crying over stupid Godzilla, or I'll get angry. Real angry. Why did the jury have to convict him and ruin my life?

I know the answer: it's because of the curse. A curse I'd do anything to fix.

CHAPTER 7

The bus passes the traffic light near the café and Harnetiaux Pets, which is pronounced "Har-na-toe." Then we stop on the north side of the creek. The freshly painted houses, giant oak trees, and green lawns make this side of Goldview look like a postcard. It helps that there's no graffiti or rusted cars. Priscilla, Jada, Curtis, and a few other kids stand up. Gigi goes with them even though she lives on the same side of the creek as me.

Priscilla heads down the aisle, and just when she's about to climb off the bus, she turns back. "Happy birthday, Sage. When I blow out my candles, I'm going to do you a favor and wish that you stay away from a life of crime."

"Haha, Priscilla," I say flatly. It's the best I can come up with. "Don't think I'm going to forget about those pickles." I narrow my eyes so she knows I mean business.

The bus drives on and Bailee bumps her shoulder against mine. "Hey, let's check out Minerva's."

"Seventh and Elm," I say. "Exactly what I'm thinking."

When we arrive at our stop on Seventh Street, we thank Mr. Melvin, climb off the bus into the oddly warm December air, and cross the intersection at Aspen Avenue.

"About Priscilla," Bailee says, launching right into her closing-arguments voice. "You can't listen to her. Ever. She's just trying to psych you out so you don't enter the Noodler contest."

"Too bad it worked." I kick a pebble and it lands about six feet up the cracked sidewalk.

"She's—"

A rumbly city bus drives past.

"What?" I say.

"She's jealous," Bailee shouts. "You're the best artist, and Priscilla is threatened."

"No, she's not. She doesn't care about art contests."

We continue up Seventh and pass Cedar Street. A few more cars drive by, but we don't need to shout anymore. "It's not about the art," Bailee says. "Priscilla doesn't want you to enter the contest because you'll win and get more attention than her, and she believes in the Contrarium Curse as much as you do. She's thinking if you become famous, then she never can."

I make a noncommittal grunt.

"Think about it!" She pushes her glasses up her nose. "Noodler is a huge deal. She's trying to make you quit before you even start."

"Maybe." I shrug. We pass a car with a flat tire and cracked windshield. I want to trust what Bailee is saying, but Godzilla did a number on my confidence. "Who cares. I don't need that contest."

"Nope. Uh-uh. We don't do that," Bailee says as we approach Elm. "You can lie to Priscilla and you can lie to everyone on the bus. But you don't lie to me."

I smile at her. "Fine." The elastic on my socks is worn out, so my socks keep bunching down into my shoe. I drop my backpack on the city bus stop bench and give them a yank.

"Hey." Bailee points across the street to a building with a maple tree next to it. "There's Minerva's."

Minerva's is a *teeeeeny*-tiny building. It's so small, we'd easily pass it if it weren't painted bright lavender. It's the only newly painted thing in this neighborhood, unless you count the streaks of black graffiti on the building next door.

We hurry across the intersection.

Minerva's windows are sparkly, and the door is shiny and red, which is an odd color to paint on a lavender building, but somehow it works. Also, instead of being a metal rectangle covered with security bars like all the other doors on this street, Minerva's door has an arched top. The upper half has twelve panels of sparkly glass and the bottom half is made out of wood with carved moons and stars like what's on the flyer.

"Sort of looks like the entrance to the witch's cottage in Hansel and Gretel," I whisper.

"Yeah." Bailee makes a big swallowing sound and says, "Why are we whispering?"

"I don't know."

Green ivy trails around a flashy lightbulb sign that reads "Minerva's."

"What was here before?" Bailee asks.

"Beats me. Come on." I pull open the heavy wooden door. A little bell chimes over my head, but for the life of me I can't see any bells.

"*Mmmmmm*," Bailee says. The smell of vanilla and exotic spices wafts around us. Sunflower-yellow walls plus the bright front windows make the store extra cheery, even though the narrow aisles are packed and piled so high it feels like things could tumble down at any second.

There's no rhyme or reason for what Minerva sells or where things are placed. Cases of leather shoelaces are stacked next to a shelf of silver yo-yos. Purple paper clips are scattered beside a crystal bowl filled with strawberry ChapSticks. Next to that sits a brown wicker basket towered high with toffees, chocolates, and boxes of mac and cheese.

On the endcap, next to a stack of electronic toys called Spheros, there are Magic Markers, flamingo floaties, and cake mixes.

"Here we go." I grab a box labeled "German chocolate." It says it comes with a free frosting packet. "Perfect."

Bailee's breathing sounds strained and noisy. Have I mentioned that Bailee doesn't like small spaces?

"Full breaths, Bay. Count it out," I say. "Inhale for four, three, two, one. Hold it."

She does.

"Now exhale for four, three, two, one."

We repeat this a few times. Bailee leans up against some unopened cases labeled "lizard food." She plunges her hand into the side pocket of her backpack and takes out her emergency hand sanitizer, the special pink pomegranate gel she saves for extraordinary occasions only. Even though the glossy floor in Minerva's doesn't have a speck of dust, Bailee dumps gel into her hands and offers a glob to me. I accept, and we rub the fruity smell into our palms.

"It's okay if you want to wait outside while I find the clerk to ring me up."

Bailee shakes her head. Her voice quavers. "There's no way I'm leaving you here alone." She follows me to the refrigerated case at the back of the store and talks herself through breaths. "Inhale." She pauses for four seconds. "Exhale."

The refrigerated case could almost qualify as organized. It has small cartons of chocolate milk, strawberry milk, and coffee milk. But it also has Scotch tape, lemon drops, and a bowl of buttons like the one Mrs. Rimmels wore that reads "Be Kind."

Running water and humming sounds echo from the back room.

I clear my throat as a courtesy to let whoever is back there know we're here.

"I'll be with you in a minute," a happy voice calls back.

"Thank you!"

Bailee and I return to the front of the store and wait by the shiny brass cash register. It's tall and old-looking, with round numbers and no digital parts.

Peppermint candies are stuffed into a glass flower vase on the counter. "I'm dying to see who owns this place," Bailee says.

"Me too." An afghan hangs over a chair behind the

counter and an unfinished crossword puzzle sits next to the register—old-people stuff. "You hear of any kids at school with a grandma named Minerva?"

Giggles explode from behind me. "I'm not a grandma," says a bubbly voice. "I'm only twenty-two in mortal years."

"Uh . . . mortal years?" Bailee and I say together.

"Haha, just kidding! That's just something I like to say." The woman is tall and thin with flowing red hair, eyes as silvery blue as a dragonfly, and small freckles dotted across her nose.

Bailee sidles closer to me.

"Now, where are my manners?" The woman clears her throat. "Howdy! I'm Minerva," she says, sing-songy, and I swear some faraway bells jingle. "That's what you guys say here in the West, right? 'Howdy.' Did I sound authentic? I've been practicing my Rocky Mountain talk all week long."

"Um, you sound great," I say. "People in Goldview rarely say 'howdy,' though. 'Hi' would be fine."

"Good to know."

"Where did you move here from?" Bailee asks.

"Oh!" She winks. "From far, *far* away."

She is odd, I think.

Bailee tilts her head.

"But enough about me. How may I help you?"

Suddenly, Minerva claps her hands and squeals. "Did you hear that? I sound like a real shop owner. This is my first assignment . . . I mean, store. And I said it. Just like that. *How may I help you?* I love the way that rolled off my tongue. Makes me want to buy some dancing boots."

A pair of cornflower-blue cowboy boots with white stitching poke out from below Minerva's long, flowy skirt.

"I like the boots you're already wearing," I say.

Minerva's eyes widen as if seeing the boots for the first time. "Oh! Yes! Me too!" She giggles and I swear those far-off bells chime again.

Bailee scrunches her brows. Maybe she noticed the bells, too.

Minerva takes the box of cake mix from my hands. "One German chocolate cake. Excellent choice. What else may I help you find? Wait! Don't tell me." She leans in close. "It'll be more fun if I guess." Minerva places a hand on her chin and studies Bailee and me for a moment. "Let's see. I have Jujubes and gummy bears."

My jaw drops. It's probably a lucky guess that she just named our two favorite candies in the whole wide world.

"Or books!" She walks to a set of shelves I hadn't

noticed before, though I don't know how I could've missed them. Rows and rows of books are lined up by color and size. There's a section of red and orange, then yellow, green, blue, indigo, and violet.

"You like how I've arranged the books?" Minerva says, her face brightening. "If you sweep your gaze quickly, you'll see a rainbow!" She touches the indigo row. "The graphic novels go here, the sci-fi in the orange, oh, and fantasy novels are shelved in sunshine yellow." Then—and I'm not lying—she twirls. "I also have everything ever written by Sarah Mlynowski, Bruce Coville, Henry Lien, Philip Pullman, Linda Sue Park, and Ingrid Law." She plucks one book after another off the shelf.

Bailee jerks her head toward me and whispers, "How does she know the names of our favorite authors?"

Minerva is suddenly standing in front of us and says to Bailee, "Perhaps you'd like some peaches-and-cream hand soap. It smells delicious and was developed at Johns Hopkins University, where they incorporated the latest in what scientists understand about antimicrobials."

Bailee's eyes widen.

"Ummm, actually," I say before Bailee tries to convince me to spend all my money on soap, "just the cake mix, please."

"Of course," Minerva says. "Let's see, those are located between the Spheros and the markers, or the Spheros and the floaties. I'll go check." She starts gliding down the aisle.

"Excuse me," I call to her back. "You already put it in a bag, remember? German chocolate?"

"Yes, yes, yes! Of course I did." She skips back to the cash register. "Anything else?"

"No, thank you."

The mix costs five bucks, which means after tax I won't have enough for a pack of candles, too.

"It's Sage's birthday today." Bailee smiles. "That's why we're baking a cake."

"Happy birthday! Do you have candles?" Minerva says, like she's reading my mind. A huge smile spreads across her face. "Can't have a birthday without candles, you know."

I realize that even though I can't afford a *whole box* of candles, this shop sells oddities, so I take a chance. "Actually, I just need to buy one candle. Do you sell single candles?"

"Do I sell single candles?" Minerva giggles like it's the funniest thing she's ever heard. "I do not sell single candles, silly-willy."

It was a dumb question. I drop my chin. A really dumb question.

Minerva finishes giggling and says, "I only give

them away. And I only give them to girls or boys celebrating a birthday, and you happen to be one. Correct?"

I lift my chin. "Really?"

She giggles again. "Some would say single candles are my specialty, and probably the most extraordinary thing in this shop. Especially when it's the twelfth candle. You wouldn't happen to be turning twelve today, would you?"

My mouth goes dry. "Uh-huh, yes."

"At eleven fifty-nine p.m." Bailee laughs. "To be precise."

"Wonderful," Minerva says. "Wait right here. I'll be back in a jiffy." She skips down the aisle, talking over her shoulder. "I just need to open the safe."

"The safe?" Bailee and I say together.

"Naturally!" Minerva hollers from the back of the store. "Twelfth candles can't be set out on the shelves for just anybody to snap up."

"They can't?" I holler back.

Bailee lifts an eyebrow.

"No sir-ree." Minerva's voice echoes from the office. "Twelfth candles are only and singularly for individuals turning twelve. Certainly, you must realize twelve is the most special birthday."

"It is?" I say.

We hear some crashing and boxes falling and Minerva saying, "Whoops! Yikes! Oyyeeeks!"

"Are you okay?" I say. "Do you need a hand?"

"Nope. I'm fine. I'm absotively fine."

Bailee loops her arm in mine. "This is strange," she whispers.

"I know," I whisper back. "I sort of love it."

"Me too!"

Minerva comes glide-skipping up the aisle with a single mint-green candle in her hand. It's skinny and probably as tall as a new pencil. "Yep, twelve is the most special year. You know why, right?"

We shake our heads.

"It's because twelve is when you're in the in-between." Minerva steps behind the cash register and reaches under the counter. She takes out a pair of scissors, a roll of lavender silk ribbon, and a long silver box. She lifts the lid off the box and places the green candle on the cushion inside it.

"The in-between?" Bailee and I say together.

"That's right." Minerva's words come out like bubbles, all joy and laughter. "Twelve is the birthday when you're in between the sweet innocence of childhood and the dynamic energy of the teenage years." Minerva's laughter stops, and her face grows serious for the first time. "The twelfth year is the most enchanted year of all, because it's during this time that you can harness the magic of the in-between." Her eyes glint. "Of course, you'd need a candle like this one to bind the magic to your wishes."

Tight laughter squeezes from my throat. "Magic?" She is definitely nutso.

Bailee's giggles sound as awkward as mine.

Minerva remains serious. "Yes, magic." She tucks something under the cushion in the silver box, places the lid on top, and rubs her hands together. Then she waves them over the box and says, "By the power vested in me, I, Minerva Beillini, bequeath my gift to Sage . . . What's your last name?"

The air feels charged, and I think I hear thunder crackling somewhere in the far, *far* distance.

"Um . . . Sassafras," I say.

Minerva blinks. Her lips curl into a smile. "By the power vested in me, I bequeath this candle to Sage Sassafras." She meets my eyes and says, "This is your special birthday candle, Sage, and yours alone. One candle, for one girl. Do you understand?"

I gulp. I may believe in curses, but not magic candles, and I definitely don't understand her. But the charged air buzzes, and I nod.

"Of course, there are wishing guidelines," Minerva says.

"Oh?" Bailee stands a little straighter. Have I mentioned how much Bailee loves rules?

Minerva ties the box with the lavender ribbon and rattles off a bunch of instructions. "You may have three wishes today, and one wish every day thereafter until the solstice, except there's no wishing on Saturdays or Sundays—those are days of rest." She smiles and says, "And don't get greedy—there's no wishing for extra candles, extra wishes, extra days, or extra wax. You hear me?" She twirls the lavender ribbon in a series of loops.

"Um?"

"Also, there's no *unwishing* a wish and no wishing to undo someone's free will. If you break any of these rules, you deactivate the candle."

"Deactivate it?" Bailee says.

"Yes, and keep in mind, Sage, if the candle is lit, you must make a wish before blowing it out, otherwise that will deactivate the candle, too, naturally." Minerva curls the ribbon in another fancy twist. "Let's see, what else—oh! Yes, and wishes must be wished by sunset on the winter solstice."

"By next Friday?" Bailee asks.

"That's right. All wishes must be made by four thirty-nine p.m. on December twenty-first, which gives you seven days. Of course, if you break the rules or use up the candle wax before the solstice, the magic is finished. And . . ."

That's one too many make-believe rules for me, so I tune out. I watch as Minerva uses her silver scissors to snip the ends of the ribbon. When she finishes the final touches on the bow, she walks out from behind the counter, hands Bailee the bag with the cake mix, and says, "It's on the house."

She turns to me and places the silver box in my palms like she's delivering a fragile egg. Minerva cups her hands around mine, looks into my eyes, and says, "Happy birthday, Sage Sassafras. Please use this well and be kind." Her voice turns singsongy. "Also remember, if you don't do what needs to be done before the solstice, you'll have to wait another generation."

"Wait another generation for what?" Bailee asks.

Minerva laughs, so we laugh, too, but Bailee and I have no idea what we're laughing about.

Bailee quiets and says, "I'm sorry, what does that mean?"

Minerva grins like we're all in on a joke. "Girls, girls, so many questions." A phone rings in the back room. "Ta-ta," she says. "Wish wisely."

CHAPTER 8

Bailee and I talk the whole walk home, amped about Minerva's strange store and the "magic" candle. It doesn't matter that it's all pretend; it's fun to dream about. I twirl and say, "I'm going to wish for a new car for my momma, and for an art kit, *and* I'm going to wish that I win the Noodler contest!"

"As your future lawyer," Bailee says, smiling, "yes on the car and art kit, no on Noodler." She skips forward and kicks a pebble. "You're going to win that contest fair and square."

"Okay. Then I'll wish for a house . . . a house with a slide from my bedroom to a chef-sized kitchen, and it'll have two refrigerators full of food and . . . wait—forget

I said house, I'll ask for a castle!"

"I love it! How about a trip to Disneyland," Bailee says, "and a treehouse, and a mountain of gummy bears?"

"Yes! I'll wish for all that!"

"Minerva was interesting, right?" Bailee says. "What do you think she meant by doing what needs to be done by the solstice?"

"I don't know. Who cares?" I laugh. "I'm going to wish for a puppy for me, a guinea pig for Momma, and for world peace—oh, and that I become a better basketball player than Priscilla so I can dunk in her face like how she always does to me. And I'm going to wish that Priscilla's parents suddenly want to move so that Priscilla has to go to a new school." I wonder if the Contrarium Curse would end if Priscilla lived a thousand miles away.

We pass under a canopy of yellow leaves. The sun slants and starts to dip behind the mountainside.

"According to the rules," Bailee says, "you can't wish for world peace, and you can't wish that Priscilla's parents want to move. You're not allowed to mess with free will."

Bailee cracks me up—talking about rules in the middle of our make-believe magic conversation. Still, I go on, "I'm going to wish that our cafeteria serves real Italian lasagna and bakery cake and that they add cartons of Cherry Garcia ice cream next to the free frozen yogurt machine." I grab the thin white trunk of an aspen tree and spin around it. "I'm going to wish for a whole bedroom makeover, and I'm going to wish that I can fly like a superhero!"

"Whoa, don't go crazy on me!" Bailee laughs.

"Do you think if I wished to be a superhero, it would automatically come with stronger muscles, or are those separate wishes?" I step on a pinecone and it makes a satisfying crunch.

"Hmmm." Bailee puts on her lawyer face and considers the validity of my wish question like she's thinking about the gazillion tiny words in a contract. "Probably a package deal."

"Oh my gosh. I'm the worst friend ever! All I've talked about are wishes for me. What do you want? What can I wish for that's just for you?"

"Really?" Bailee stops walking. "The candle is not like a never-ending bank account."

I laugh. "Whatever. You're my best friend. If this thing were real I'd make wishes for you, so come on. What do you want?" I hook my elbow in hers, and we walk up to the mailboxes at my apartment building, a big metal square with thirty small doors.

"Hmmm," Bailee says. "I'd like the bedroom make-over wish, too."

"Done," I say. "One Pottery Barn Teen room for

you and one for me! What else?"

I let go of Bailee's arm and open the mail slot that belongs to Momma and me. I pull out a couple of past-due notices and a thin white envelope with my name on it. The return address has that familiar, boxy government stamp: FCI, 9595 WEST QUINCY AVENUE, LITTLETON, CO.

Bailee spins in a circle and adds to her wish list. ". . . and a horse, too."

I shove the mail under my armpit. It's not that I'm trying to hide my letter from Bailee, exactly, it's just that I'm not ready to explain that I don't want to open it yet. "FCI" stands for Federal Correctional Institution. This is my fourth letter from Daddy—one for every week he's been gone, and I feel some sort of ways I don't understand.

But I'm not going to lie. There is one emotion I do understand—I'm angry. Why did he have to be at the wrong place at the wrong time? And why didn't we ever talk about it? It's not fair. We used to work through everything. But after Daddy came home on bail, Momma cried a lot, so instead of discussing his court case and the accusations, we spent those months acting as if things were normal, even when we moved into the apartment.

I got so good at pretending that now I pretend he's

off on an important business trip or on an adventure, and these letters are actually notes from exotic places. If I don't read them, it's easier on my heart.

"Okay?" Bailee says as I tune back in. "Make it a white horse."

"Just a horse?" I force lightness into my voice. "How about a narwhal?"

"Wait, isn't that a mythological creature?"

"No, unicorns are fake. Narwhals are real."

"Perfect! I'll just need a bigger bathtub."

We both laugh and climb the stairs to my second-floor apartment.

I take the silver key from the chain around my neck, unlock the door, and flip the light switch.

Nothing happens. No light. I flip it up and down and up and down, but of course nothing changes.

"Dang it! There goes the electricity again."

My momma is really smart and gets A's on all her tests in night school—she wants to be a physical therapist—but she forgets a lot of things like groceries, putting gas in the car, and paying utilities. Xcel Energy shuts off our electricity at least three times a year. I don't mind so much in the summer, because it stays light outside until nine o'clock, but in December, the days are really short. Right now, it's only 4:20 p.m. and the sun is already starting to go down, and the worst thing about our tiny apartment is that it doesn't let in a lot of natural light.

"Dang it!" I drop the mail and my backpack on the floor and say my new crummy color. "Sepia."

"Mauve!" Bailee says, adding her own cursing color.

The leafy oak tree outside blocks most of the window light. The remaining droopy yawns of sunlight stretch through the open door. I hurry to the kitchen, set my silver candle box on the counter, and pull a flashlight from a drawer. *Click click.* "Out of batteries!"

"Mauve!" Bailee repeats.

"Here." I hand the flashlight to Bailee. "Check what size batteries we need."

Bailee unscrews the flashlight, and I squat in front of our mostly empty pantry to find the battery box. I move aside cleaning supplies, a carton of plastic garbage bags, and the framed pictures I made for Daddy when he lived with us. Some frames are wrapped in bubble wrap and others are just on the floor. Momma hasn't gotten around to buying nails, so we can't hang them yet. Behind the frames, I find the shoebox where we store new batteries.

"The flashlight needs D batteries," Bailee says.

I dig past the As, the AAAs, the square nine-volts, and even a pack of Cs. No Ds.

Bailee shuts the apartment door and the room shadows into shades of gray.

"Hey, why are you shutting the door?"

"Can't let in too many bugs, otherwise your mom will spend all night catching them to carry outside."

She's right. I shove the battery box back to its spot behind the frames and stand up. The final rays of light squeeze past the tree and in through our small front window. I pull open a kitchen drawer, take out the matches, and untie the lavender ribbon from my silver box.

"You're going to light your new birthday candle?"

"No choice." I grab the green candle from the box. "We'll be in the dark soon."

"Yeah, but . . . shouldn't you light a different one?"

I strike the match and hold it to the wick. "Nah, the others are way too short."

My new candle sizzles to life and sends a rich warm glow throughout the apartment, which includes a total of two bedrooms, one bathroom, zero hallways, and a living room that's also a dining room and kitchen all pressed into one. The yellow flame glimmers.

"Whoa," Bailee says, all breathy. "I've never seen that much light from a single candle."

"Or even a flashlight," I say, equally impressed.

"Aren't you worried about wasting it, you know,

since Minerva made it feel so special?"

I laugh. "Haha, good one."

Bailee laughs, awkward and stiff.

"I mean, it's fun dreaming about wishes, but we don't really believe in all that, right?" I say.

Bailee rubs the back of her neck. "At least we have light." The flame reflects off her glasses.

"Yeah." The room is stuffy since the apartment has been shut all day, which would not be a big deal in a normal December since Colorado is usually chilly this time of year, but Goldview's "magical" weather has delivered bonus doses of warm days. "Ugh, no electricity means no ceiling fan."

Bailee sighs. "And no cake baking, either."

"Sepia," I say, sinking into one of our three wooden kitchen chairs. I slump at the lopsided table. The flame flickers and a trail of green wax inches its way down my pointing finger and then drips onto the table.

"I'm sorry, Sage," Bailee says. "We can bake at my house if you don't mind my little brothers eating half the cake."

"Thanks." More melted wax warms my fingertips. "I sure wish Momma had paid the electric bill this time."

A rush of wind bursts out from the air vent, blowing out the candle. At the same time, the lights and ceiling fan click on.

I jump up and Bailee screams.

"Hot magenta!" I say. "Best timing ever!"

Bailee glares at the trail of smoke rising from the candle. "Sage." She crosses her arms over her stomach. "You just made a wish."

"What?"

"You just said you wished your mom paid the electric bill, and then the electricity came back on!"

"Yeah . . . I guess I did," I say. "Cool coincidence!"

"You know I am not a believer in coincidences."

"Well, this is proof you should be." I set the candle on top of our lopsided table, and Bailee snatches it up, holding it in the careful way Minerva had at the store—with reverence.

"Okay, I'm just going to say it," Bailee says. "All joking aside, I think this candle is magical."

CHAPTER 9

The oven bell dings, alerting us that the preheat is done and the temperature has reached 350 degrees. I carefully slide the cake pan inside and set the timer.

Bailee dumps the empty cake mix box into our recycling bin and puts the wax liner into the regular trash. She picks up the candle from the tile countertop. "Sage," she says in a soft voice, which tells me she is going to try again to convince me, "you made a wish, and according to Minerva, since you turn twelve today, you're officially in the in-between." She twists the candle. "I really think Minerva gave you a charmed candle or she charmed your candle or something."

"Oh, Bay. You can never tell when people are joking." I wet a sponge and focus on wiping cake mix from the counter. I don't want to let her see my hope, because hope is a dangerous thing. Last time I let it rise, the jury said "guilty" and sent Daddy away.

"I'm pretty sure Minerva wasn't joking. Why else would she give you all those rules?"

I toss the sponge into the sink. "Don't tell me you have them committed to memory."

"Yep." Bailee waves the candle like a wizard's wand and recites Minerva's rules again. "Three wishes today. No asking for more magic. No unwishing wishes."

She goes on and all I hear is, "Do this, don't do that. Blah blah blah."

Still, her sureness floats my hope to a shade of bubblegum pink, but this has to be impossible. "You're joking with me, right?" I laugh nervously.

Bailee shakes her head.

"Swear it," I say. "Swear to me on your pile of hand gels, including the pink pomegranate one, that you're not joking?"

"I was half joking before, but now I'm all in." Bailee does not bite her lip. Her face stays lawyer-level serious. "Minerva slipped something in the box. We should check it out."

She grabs the silver box, lifts the lid, and takes

out the white pillow cushion. Under it, she finds a small roll of paper. "Look!" She unrolls the paper and squints to read it.

"Well?"

Bailee clears her throat. "'No wishing on religious holidays or celebrations, including but not limited to Hanukkah, Christmas, Diwali, Muharram, Purim, Ramadan, Jan . . . Janmashtami—'"

"Okay, skip the list, I'll never remember all those."

"'Furthermore, Saturdays and Sundays are days of rest. You are allowed to pray if you so choose; however, there shall be no wishing.'"

I chuff even though belief and hope are sneaking up on me. "Yeah, Minerva already said that."

"And," Bailee's voice rises and now she's jumping up and down, "you get a bonus wish at eleven fifty-nine p.m., since that's the exact moment of your birth!"

Bailee scoops up the candle, grabs the matches, and strikes one. The flame ignites from blue to white.

"What are you doing?"

"Testing. If the candle isn't magical, then no biggie." She presses the flame to the wick and lights it. "Wish for something we can see immediately." Bailee twists the candle in her palm. In an airy voice, she adds, "Sage, Minerva wouldn't have wasted our time with so many rules if this wasn't real."

The candle flickers and the sulfur smell from the match tickles my nose.

She hands the candle to me. "Make a wish we can see right away."

"Seriously?"

"Yes! Please. What will it hurt if you just try it?" A drop of wax melts its way down the side of the candle and warms the end of my thumb.

I twist my mouth to one side and as I think and think, drop after drop trails down the mint-green stem.

"Come on!" Bailee says.

"Okay. I've got it. I wish right now I had a pepperoni pizza to eat at a non-lopsided table."

"Oh, smart!" Bailee says. "You might have just found a loophole to get two wishes in one—pizza *and* an even table."

"What?"

"A loophole! You said '*at*' a non-lopsided table instead of 'and,' so it came out as just one wish."

Bailee loves rules, but she also loves loopholes, because a loophole is a way to legally get around a rule.

Drip, drip, drip, drip, drip. Wax races down the candle.

I blow it out, and at the exact same moment, the doorbell rings.

Bailee and I jump clear to the ceiling, and I'm not going to lie, I might have peed a little, too. We run to the door and I call through the thin wooden frame, "Um . . . who is it?"

Bailee's eyes are as wide as mine feel.

"It's Tammy from next door. I have a little something for your birthday."

Miss Tammy is Momma's closest friend. When we needed an apartment, she told us about the one next to hers.

I swing open the door with a big hello ready on my lips, except Miss Tammy is holding a pizza box! Steam rises from the corners and the scent of pepperoni floats to my nose.

"This is for you," Miss Tammy says.

Bailee's hands fly over her mouth, knocking her glasses crooked.

"Blue bunny rabbits!" I scream, slam the door shut, drop to a squat, and curl my arms around my shins. "Oh my gosh! Oh my gosh! My wish just came true!"

CHAPTER 10

age?" Miss Tammy says from the other side of the door.

Bailee swings it open. "Sorry, Miss Tammy."

I stand up. "Sorry. I . . . I . . ." My mind is too buzzy to think of a lie. "Uhhh . . ." Swallow. "Thank you!"

Miss Tammy squeezes her penciled-in eyebrows together, her blue eyeliner shining extra thick under the porch light. "Are you okay, Sage?"

"Yes, ma'am. It's just a big day, turning twelve and all." I fold my arms over my stomach. "Um . . . would you like to come in?"

"I would, but I can't stay." She steps around my backpack and the scattered mail and sets the pizza on the crooked tabletop. "Goodness, your momma still hasn't fixed this table." She squats down. "Sage, come lift this side a couple of inches."

I do and Miss Tammy pushes in the wobbly leg and twists it until it tightens in place. "There we go."

Miss Tammy stands up and brushes herself off. I set down the table.

"It's not lopsided anymore!" Bailee squeals and then clamps a hand over her mouth again.

"Oh, Bay Leaf." Miss Tammy laughs. "It's just a little repair. Not a big deal." She glances at the thin gold watch squeezed around her freckled wrist. "I have to hurry in for my shift at the café. Now, come here, my little spice." She pulls me in for a tight hug, wrapping her plump arms around me. The scent of her Aqua Net hairspray fills my nose, and I return the hug, watching steam rise from the pizza box.

Miss Tammy leans back, holding me by the shoulder. She studies my face and her voice goes weepy. "Happy birthday, darling. I can't believe you're twelve today." She sniffles. "Have I ever told you I was the first person who held you when you came home from the hospital?"

"Yes, ma'am." She's only told me twelve million times, and it's made me smile twelve million times, too. I love Miss Tammy almost as much as I love my momma and daddy.

"Well of course I have." She pulls a bright dandelion-yellow envelope from her purse. "Here's your card. I'm going to go ahead and blow the surprise right now and tell you I slipped ten dollars inside. It's not a lot, but it's yours to spend however you'd like."

I hug her again. "It's too much. Thank you."

Miss Tammy laughs and checks the time on her watch again. "Alrighty, I need to scoot so I can catch that five-fifteen bus."

I nod, placing a hand on top of the warm pizza box. It's really real!

"Happy birthday, Lil' Spice. I love you."

"Love you, too."

She pops in her earbuds, and the door clicks shut behind her.

Bailee now clamps two hands over her mouth. I keep mine closed, too. I lift five fingers to the air and do a slow countdown. Five, four, three, two . . . when I get to one, Bailee and I scream.

"Holy magenta! Holy magenta! Do you see what I see?" Bailee points at the pizza box. "Of course, you see it. But do you *see* it? Oh! My! Gosh!"

I holler nonsense. "Pizza leetza feetza neatsa!" I laugh. "A pepperoni pizza! Just like that! I wished for a pepperoni pizza and here it is!"

It's our proof of magic. A pizza box on my table, the no-longer-lopsided table! And I scream, "And the table!"

"I know!" Bailee jumps up and down.

I pick up the magic candle and dance from one end of the apartment to the other, which only takes about five seconds, but still. Bailee dances behind me, both of us chanting, "Pep-per-oni pizza! Pep-per-oni pizza!"

"Thank goodness you listened to Minerva," I say, still marching and dancing. "True confession, I sort of tuned out the list of rules. Give them to me one last time."

Bailee stops and puts on her lawyer face, runs through the rules for the third time, and adds, "Since you didn't pay attention, you probably missed when Minerva said wishes are like recipes."

"Huh? Like I need ingredients or something?" I stop dancing. "Please tell me I don't have to find an eye of newt or anything horrible like that. I'm not killing any lizards."

"No! Minerva said she meant it metaphorically— her word, not mine."

"For example?" I ask.

"Like if you make a fruit salad or a turkey sandwich, you can eat it right away, it's ready to go. But if you blend up a batch of chocolate chip cookies, they take time, like ten minutes to bake, and if you make bread from scratch you have to let the dough rise and it can take all day. Each recipe has its own time frame for when it's finished baking and ready to go."

"Okay."

Even though I understand, Bailee goes on, because she loves any opportunity to use her lawyer voice.

"Therefore, some magic you'll see right away." She points at the pizza box. "And some magic will need time to bake. Speaking of which, how much longer until the cake is ready?"

The whole apartment smells like a Hershey's chocolate bar. I check the oven timer. "Twelve minutes. Now, where did you put the matches? I'm ready for a real wish!"

Bailee's hands shake as she grabs the box of matches from the end of the counter. "What are you going to wish for?"

"Art supplies, of course."

"Oh, good one." She flips down the light switch before striking the match.

"Why did you turn out the lights?"

"Atmosphere!"

The match hisses to life. I can only see her hand and some shadows until she touches the fire to the candlewick. A blue-and-yellow flame dances to life, and I swear I see lavender, too. The blaze waves back and forth and the room glows to a warm gold-yellow tone. Just when I'm about to wish for all the art supplies a girl could ever dream of, I catch sight of the mail scattered on the floor by the door—the overdue notices and the letter from my daddy. I squeeze my eyes shut, thinking about how hard my momma works and yet we still have an empty refrigerator. I think of all the lawyer fees, about empty gas tanks and unpaid electric bills. Another drop of wax warms the tip of my finger, and I say, "I wish someone would give Momma a bunch of money."

Drip, drip, drip, drip, drip, drip, drip, drip, drip, drip, drip, drip.

Wax trails down the candle and it shrinks. I blow it out.

"Whoa!" Bailee says. "Did you see how much wax just disappeared?"

I hold up the candle. Now it's about three inches tall. "Must be the bigger the wish, the more wax it takes away?"

"Hmmm." Bailee's face scrunches. "Would have been nice to know that rule up front."

"I still would've made that wish." But the moment those words leave my mouth I realize my mistake. "Wait. No! Shoot! I actually made the wrong wish."

"What do you mean?" Bailee says, pushing her

glasses up her nose.

"Call your mom and see if you can stay the night! I still have that bonus wish at eleven fifty-nine."

While Bailee calls, I grab a warm slice of cheesy pizza and sink my teeth into the pepperonis.

A moment later, Bailee is all smiles. The slumber party is a go. She grabs plates and paper towels for us, helps herself to a slice, and presses me to find out what I'm going to wish for.

Since she doesn't understand the curse, and I'm not ready to put my thoughts into words, I tell her she'll have to wait. She's patient—unlike me—so she's good at waiting.

I chomp into my second slice of pizza and ask, "How long do you think it'll take for the money wish to come true?"

"No clue." Bailee wipes cheese from her mouth.

We keep talking about wishes and eating pizza until the oven timer dings, and we take the cake out. I break off a couple of tiny bits of cake for Bailee and me to eat right away. Bailee rolls her eyes at me, but she eats her cake. We let the rest of the cake cool and then frost and top it with just eleven candles, the regular ones. According to the rules, I've already made my three wishes, so I can't light the special candle for the bonus wish until 11:59.

We talk about Minerva's and wishes all evening,

and several hours later, Momma comes home with tired-looking eyes. "Hi, Bailee. Happy birthday, Sage." She comes over to the couch and hugs me tight, the sweat of the day still on her, but I don't mind. "Did you have a good day?"

"Yep!" I wag my eyebrows at Bailee. "Miss Tammy brought pizza."

Momma grabs a slice of cold pizza and joins us on the couch. I won't tell her about Minerva's, but I consider telling her about the Noodler contest. Problem is, she's usually too tired to talk at night. Sure enough, she scoops up the remote and clicks on the television. The three of us scoot close on the couch, our legs curling underneath us, and we laugh as we watch a sitcom.

After the show ends, Momma and Bailee sing happy birthday to me. I blow out the eleven candles, the ones that don't hold any real magic, and we eat cake and watch more TV. Momma showers and goes to bed around 10:30. Bailee and I go in my room and try to fix the chips in our purple nail polish. Then we lay our heads on our pillows and talk more about Minerva's. We set an alarm so we won't miss the wishing minute.

At 11:55 p.m., the alarm goes off. Momma is sound asleep. The apartment is dark except for a single nightlight over the oven. Bailee and I tiptoe to the kitchen, the tile cool on our bare feet. "I don't see money any-where," I whisper. Our shadows silhouette the wall.

"A money wish must be the kind that requires lon-ger baking time," Bailee says. "Trust the process."

"Okay." I slide open the kitchen drawer, take out my magic candle, and stick it in the half-eaten cake.

"What's your big secret wish?" Bailee says.

"When I made the money wish, I was thinking about how rough Momma has it."

"Yeah?"

"And how easy the Pettys have it."

"Yeah?"

"So, what I really should have wished for is the curse to finally turn in my momma's favor." I take out the matches.

"A curse-reverse?" Bailee's eyes widen.

"Yep. A curse-reverse covers all good things and will grant me several wishes in one—Momma will become more responsible, we'll stop living poor, and the best part is, the judge will figure out the jury got it wrong, so my daddy can get out of jail."

"Well, but—" Bailee lifts a hand to her chin.

"Nope. Don't try talking me out of it."

The clock ticks to 11:59. I strike a flame and light the candle. Yellow, blue, and lavender dance across the kitchen walls. Bailee grabs my hands and squeezes them for good luck. I look her in the eyes and say, "I wish the Contrarium Curse would flip on its head."

A gazillion drips of wax shorten my enchanted green candle to only an inch and a half tall.

I blow it out and smile.

The wish cost me half the candle, but I know it's going to be worth it.

How could it not be?

CHAPTER 11
SATURDAY, DECEMBER 15

On Saturday morning, I shake Bailee by the shoulder. "Wake up. Let's see if there's a bag of money on the table!" Seeing the money wish come true will assure me the curse-reverse is up next. Bailee throws on her glasses, and we rush out of my room. There's no money in the living room/kitchen/dining room.

"Bummer," I say, sinking into a chair at the table.

Momma is not around, either. Her purse isn't on the hook by the door, and her favorite yellow teacup sits on the wooden tabletop, empty other than the dried-out teabag at the bottom.

"Don't worry," Bailee says. "The money and the

curse-reverse are probably two wishes that take extra baking time and patience."

"You really think they'll come true?"

"Absolutely. The rules say so."

I run a finger over the chip in Momma's cup and carry it to the kitchen. Dirty mixing bowls and dishes with dried cake crumbs and pizza sauce tower in the sink. I dump a glob of yellow liquid Dawn into the basin and turn on warm water. It smells like lemons.

Bailee crunches the pizza box into the trash can.

"We're out of cereal," I say. "That means cake for breakfast."

"Perfect!"

Sudsy water inches its way up the sink. "Or you can have the can of Pringles in the pantry."

"I'll pass. Where's your mom?"

"I don't kn—"

The front door swings open and in walks Momma. "Hello, girls!" Her hair is swept up into a ponytail and a few loose strands frame her small face.

In one hand, she has our canvas grocery bag. It's full, with carrots and oranges poking out from the top. In the other, she's carrying a present!

Score!

Momma toting a bag of groceries and a gift is enough to make me believe the money wish must have come true.

The present is wrapped in my favorite color paper, dioxazine purple, and it's topped with a giant red bow. Other years, when Momma gave me a gift, she'd wrapped it in a napkin or paper placemat from the café, and I'm not complaining, it's just the reason why my mouth is hanging open now.

"Hey, Momma!"

"Happy birthday, sweet pea! I'm sorry I didn't have this for you yesterday." She puts the present on our wooden table and joins Bailee and me by the sink, setting the Sprouts bag on the counter and kissing me on the cheek. Today, instead of smelling like the factory, she smells like her mango hair conditioner.

"Thanks!" I turn off the faucet and drop the sponge in the water.

"May I help you with anything?" Bailee is already unloading the pancake mix and a pint of raspberries from the bag.

"Um, hellooooo." I scoop up a handful of bubbles and blow them at Bailee. "There is a gift with my name on it, and I'm about to open it. Right, Momma?"

Momma laughs. "That's what I'm thinking!" Lately, I've been searching for ways that Momma and I are alike—here's one: neither of us ever want to delay fun.

I rush to the table and tear through the purple wrapping, screaming, "Yes-yes-yes!" It's a sketch pad and an artist's set of Prismacolor pencils. The pencils are made of cedar and have super-awesome colors—dragon-scale blue, hummingbird green, fairy-tale pink, Mars dust red, you name it. "Best! Gift! Ever!" I say.

"I slipped a few sheets of artist paper in your sketch pad," Momma says, "for special projects."

"Everything you need for the contest, Sage!" Bailee says.

Infamous to famous, here I come!

I hug Momma. "Thank you!"

She laughs. "What contest?"

I finally tell her about Doodle for Noodler.

Momma takes my hands. "Let me know if you need anything else, okay?"

There's no way I am going to tell her about all the fancy computer programs the kids on the bus talked about. "Thank you, Momma. This is perfect."

"Paints or brushes or whatever you need, no problem. I have a genius get-rich scheme." Momma laughs at herself.

"Oh yeah?" I dart a peek at Bailee to see if she's thinking about the money wish, too.

"Well, 'rich' might be a stretch." Momma laughs again. "But we have a little bit of extra money. I sold a few odds and ends at Re-Bay, and I just dropped off a few more items."

"What's Re-Bay?" Bailee asks.

"Re-Bay sells items on eBay for people who don't want to deal with the selling part, like figuring out the pricing, or how to post your ad, or dealing with the customers, packaging, and shipping, all that. You just drop off whatever you want to get rid of and Re-Bay does it all and then keeps a small percentage of the money."

"What did you sell?" I ask.

"This first time," Momma says, "I sold a purse and a few jackets I haven't worn in years."

I dart a look at the door and then around the table and realize the leather purse Daddy gave Momma, the one she took such good care of, is nowhere in sight.

"Your purse!"

"Oh, hush," she says. "Your dad would want you to have art supplies. Plus, who needs a purse when I have the Sprouts bag?"

"Thank you so much." I slide out a kitchen chair and spread my new supplies across the table. "Do you guys mind if I practice drawing Noodler logos?"

"Go for it," Bailee says.

"Would you like to help me make pancakes, Bailee?" Momma asks.

"I'd love to!"

I open the box of pencils. They are already sharpened, their weight perfect. First, I practice with the sketching pencil. It glides across the paper's thick grain in such a satisfying way that I lose myself, and before I know it, I've drawn our school bus with Mr. Melvin driving and Bay and me sitting nine rows down on the right. Then I draw the Noodler logo like pavers in the road.

I flip to a new page and test the colored pencils, each one floating across the rich paper. I switch back to the sketch pencil and use more pages to write "Noodler" over and over again, creating different fonts and styles and changing the logo letters into an image of some things in my life: an N-shaped apartment complex, two O chocolate donuts.

The apartment fills with the smell of pancakes and melting butter. Mmmmmm.

I take the Mars dust red pencil from the box and draw the *D*. It looks like a *D* but also a pair of lips tilted sideways, because the red reminds me of Miss Tammy's lipstick. The hummingbird green isn't the same color as my magic candle, but I still use it to shape the *L* into a candle. I add a yellow-and-lavender flame. The *E* is the best part; it's a sideways version of me, Momma, and Daddy holding hands.

"Sage," Momma says, suddenly sitting beside me.

I look up. Bailee is by the stove, flipping pancakes. Momma slides an envelope toward me, the one from yesterday, marked up by the Federal Correctional Institution. "I found this on the floor."

I stare at the letter. I forgot to hide it in my dresser drawer with the others. My mouth dries. "Oh."

"It might be a birthday note," she says gently.

"Yeah." I'm quiet.

If Daddy were here, he'd see the questions I have but don't know how to ask. Momma and I don't know how to talk about Daddy, or anything, really.

But Momma surprises me. She touches my hand and says, "I know it's your daddy who you spoke to about hard things. But now that he's . . ." She takes a breath. "If you need to talk, I am here for you."

I nod and swallow down words I haven't even figured out. Words that aren't ready. We both look at my drawing, me focused on the *E*. Three people holding hands.

That'll be my family once the curse-reverse completes and my daddy is sprung from jail.

CHAPTER 12

At noon, Momma drops off Bailee and me at the dollar theater.

"Make sure you get gas for the car," I tell her before shutting the door.

"Oh, Sage." Momma shakes her head like I'm being ridiculous, but she has to know I'm right, since she's forgotten before.

The car rattles as she drives off, and Bailee and I head inside to see the matinee double of *Star Wars* movies—*A New Hope* and *The Empire Strikes Back*—Bailee's treat for my birthday. The theater smells like buttery popcorn, and even though I have ten dollars plus a few quarters in my back pocket, Bailee uses her money and buys each of us our own bag of gummy bears.

After the movies, Momma is twenty-five minutes late picking us up, which is fine since it's another sunny day, and the sky is a rich shade of Maya blue. Bailee and I use the time to practice cartwheels on the soft grass outside. But Momma's tardiness also tells me the curse-reverse hasn't started working yet.

When Momma pulls up, we climb into the car, and Bailee pushes her hand gel my way.

"Really?" I say.

"Hello! Bug larvae!" she says. "You never know what we touched in that grass."

I'm rubbing in the gel when a Mimi Glosser song comes on the radio. Momma cranks the volume, and the three of us sing at the top of our lungs with the windows down, our hair blowing every which way. We laugh and sing to the next song, too. Momma is fun like that. Ten minutes later, we arrive at Bailee's house. "Good seeing you, Bailee," Momma says. "Tell your parents hello."

"I will, Mrs. Sassafras. Thank you for the ride." Bailee closes the car door.

We wait and watch Bailee walk to her porch, and a single gold leaf floats down from a sugar maple tree. It flutters through the window, landing on Momma's lap. The leaf is huge and perfect, and it's more than just gold, it has shades of tiger orange and fire yellow, too. Momma picks it up by the stem. "Will you look at this." Her voice fills with wonder. "The first leaf I've seen fall this year."

"Odd, right?" I say.

Bailee waves before going inside. I wave back.

"Nobody has ever heard of autumn leaves in Colorado in the middle of December," Momma says. "More proof that Goldview's weather is magical."

Her mention of magic makes me look at her more closely—suntanned cheeks, heart-shaped face, and those bright hazel eyes. Mine are dark brown like Daddy's, but I realize the almond shape of her eyes is like mine. The skin on my neck tingles. I sense a new spark between Momma and me, a sign that maybe we can do more than sing and laugh and watch TV. Maybe I can find words to talk to her about what's been on my mind. Since breakfast, the idea of talking has been spinning in my stomach. Only problem is, I don't know how to start.

I look at the leaf and clear my throat. "It's pretty."

"We'll save it and press it into a book." Momma sets it down between us, like a bridge from her to me. She grinds the car into gear, and it rattles as we back out of the driveway.

The street is edged with green spruces and trees full of leafy branches with shades of golden brown, vermilion red, and honey yellow. A soft breeze blows pine through our windows, and the rustling leaves sound like a whisper. *The solstice is coming.* My arm hairs spike. What did Minerva want me to do by sunset on the solstice?

A few more leaves trickle down as we zoom past.

"How was the movie?"

"Awesome!" I mimic Darth Vader. "No, *I* am your father."

Momma laughs. "Your daddy can do the Darth Vader voice, too. You're just like him."

"No, I'm not!" flies out of my mouth before I can stop it.

Momma whips a look at me before taking a breath. "What's wrong?" Her voice is soft. "You used to like it when I'd say that."

"I didn't mean to sound ugly, but . . . maybe I'm more like you than him?"

"Okay?" she says, her face screwing up like she's confused.

I want to tell her that my anger at Daddy confuses me, too, but the words stay trapped in my mouth.

I clear my throat for the second time, struggling to catch the enchanted vibe between us before it slips away. I have questions about Daddy. About the trial. About us. About the things we never talk about. I want to say I never tell her stuff because she overreacts. I'm ready to talk and now feels like a better moment than ever, so I start with, "I know the jury got it wrong." I wait for a reaction. Neither one of us has ever said those words out loud before.

Momma stays quiet. Maybe she's waiting for me to finish, so as gentle as possible I add, "It's just that . . . even though he didn't do it, Daddy is technically a convicted thief and because of that, everyone in town thinks we're thieves, too."

I pick at the purple nail polish on my thumb and wait. Here's Momma's chance to holler, "People are dumb, the jury was dumb, and they got it wrong!" And then I'll hug her and say, "Let's take it to the Supreme Court!" or something like what they say on TV, and we'll get fired up together and figure out what to do next.

Or if Momma doesn't say that, she might say something helpful the way Daddy would if he were here, like ideas on how to deal with the snide looks at school and Godzilla's comments, or she'll tell me that I'm going to win the Noodler contest and become so famous that nobody will ever be a jerk to me again.

But Momma doesn't do any of these things. All she

adds is, "People don't think we're thieves." She doesn't sound sure or even surprised.

I'm determined to keep trying to talk, and so I uncork another bit of news. "Gigi stopped being my friend because of Daddy's arrest."

"Is that why she's not coming around?" Momma takes a quick glance at me, making the car swerve.

"She hasn't exactly said that out loud, but I know that's why she stopped hanging out with me."

"I'll call her mother just as soon as we get home."

"No!" My ears turn hot. This is exactly why I never tell her stuff. "I don't want you fixing this, that would be humiliating."

Momma huffs.

"Momma! I'm just telling you about how things are. Promise me you won't call."

She slows at a yield sign and releases a sigh. "Fine. Whatever Gigi thinks doesn't matter anyhow. Here's what important for you to remember about your daddy, Sage. He loves you, and I do, too."

"Okay." I say it in surrender, because why bother. Momma doesn't understand, or she doesn't want to. My stomach stops spinning even though I finally know the words I wish I could say—that ever since Daddy was accused, arrested, and convicted, I've gone from regular Sage to everyone looking at me like I'm

Aladdin, the street rat, or Ponyboy, the gutter kid. Things have been lousy—losing our house, losing Gigi, and dealing with kids who worry I might snatch their lunch money. Added to that, Daddy's conviction gives Godzilla more ammunition than is fair in a family feud.

I stuff those words underneath my rib cage, putting them in prison, too.

"You know what? You're right!" Momma smiles, not noticing or maybe ignoring the unspoken stuff. "You *are* like me. Like how you couldn't wait to open your present."

I nod, but all I can think of are the ways I'm not like her, because even though Momma doesn't know how to talk to me, she has an easy heart for Daddy. She reads his letters. She takes his Sunday phone calls. She stays positive and tells him she loves him, and the way her voice sounds, I can tell she means it.

Problem with me and these phone calls is, I love my daddy. I love him so much I'm afraid questions will jump out of my mouth, and he'll know what I'm thinking, because even though I say my daddy didn't do it, sometimes I wonder if he did.

It's why those letters buried in my drawer are scary to think about.

"... and maybe you should talk to her about it."

"What?" I say.

"Gigi," Momma says. "You should talk to her."

"There's nothing to talk about. She's Team Priscilla, now."

"Well—but . . ."

"Momma, you don't know how middle school works these days."

"I want to understand." She touches my hand, and for a moment my heart hopes she'll say more and prove to me she does get it. Daddy was good at hearing the things I didn't say. But Momma settles on, "I'm sorry, honey."

I shrug. "It's okay." As soon as I say that, I realize "okay" is possible, because the curse-reverse can fix everything, including my friendship with Gigi. I cross my fingers and slide them under my legs.

The road winds left and right, and I come up with an idea of what we should do next. "Can we go to the Harnetiaux pet store?"

Momma's body stiffens. "You know I don't like to go to stores around here."

I throw my arms up. "You just told me it's not true that everyone in town thinks we're thieves, but you don't want to go anywhere anymore, because you think people are whispering about you, and maybe they are but—"

"I'm sorry, Sage. It's hard for me."

It's hard for me, too, I think, but keep my lips zipped, because Momma deals with enough, and her facing townsfolk is probably as hard as me facing school. You never know when someone's going to slip a pickle on your seat.

We stop at a four-way intersection, and a coal-black Tesla pulls to the stop sign directly across from us. It's Priscilla and her mother.

Momma grips the steering wheel so hard her knuckles turn white. She eases her foot on the gas pedal and, *putter, putter, pfloop.* A puff of gray rises from our car and we stop moving.

Mrs. Petty waves as her car glides silently past, Godzilla laughing in the passenger seat.

I want to tell Momma that I'd like to fill up Mrs. Petty's entire car with pickles, but I keep those words buried, too.

"I should've gone for the fancy cars in the curse, huh?" Momma says with a small laugh, trying to restart the engine with no luck.

"Did you run out of gas?"

"No, Sage. We're having engine troubles. I just need to let them get some distance. You know my car acts up whenever I'm near Candice Petty." Momma waits a moment before turning the key again. The car rattles to life and she pats the dashboard. "See." She clicks on her blinker. "You know what? We can go."

"Huh?" I turn to face her.

"It's your birthday weekend. Pet store, here we come." Her voice lightens. "But we are only going to look. Re-Bay is not going to bring in enough cash to feed another mouth right now."

"Really?" As soon as I realize I'm getting my way, I feel bad because I've guilted her into it. And now I'm stressed because I know she was worried about one real possibility—in this town, you never know who you're going to run into.

CHAPTER 13

We pull into the parking lot where a man on a ladder works on the Harnetiaux Pets sign.

Momma parks at the end spot and turns off the engine.

"Ready?" I open my door.

Instead of opening her door, too, she scans the store windows, doing her usual search to see if any of the town gossips are inside. Sure enough, she spots someone. "I'm going to wait in the car."

"Momma," I say in a plea, trying to see who she sees, "you could visit the guinea pigs."

She considers this for a moment. When Daddy was home, we'd come to Harnetiaux Pets at least once a month because Daddy and I liked volunteering with the rescue dogs. While we walked the rescues and played with them, Momma spent her time with the guinea pigs, holding them, naming them, even rearranging their cages. Daddy always wanted to buy one for her, but she refused. Daddy explained it was because the first guinea pig Momma ever owned had been a gift from Mrs. Petty—a best-friend gift. So when the snake ate the pup and their friendship ended, it must've felt like the worst kind of betrayal. He couldn't say for sure, though, since Momma's not the best at sharing her feelings.

She turns her attention back to the store window. "No." She shakes her head like she's underlining her "no." "Mrs. Snyder from the bank is in there, and I can't deal with her."

"But—"

"Mr. Harnetiaux is a sweetheart, but I'm not up for that Snyder woman. Sorry."

"Momma," I whine.

"Go on. Take your time," she says sweetly. "Play with the puppies, pet the cats. It's gorgeous outside. I'm going to sit here with the windows down and read my book." She takes a novel from the seat pocket behind her and opens it up.

I sigh. But I understand, since Mrs. Snyder is one of

Momma's very own Godzillas.

Thinking of Godzilla's smirky little face laughing at me and Momma makes my blood boil. Godzilla, the bully. Godzilla, the fraidy-cat of crickets. Godzilla, who I owe for the pickle incident. Godzilla, who deserves my revenge. I pause. I have an idea. The perfect idea! A prank that will teach Priscilla once and for all not to mess with me.

I grab the Sprouts bag from the back seat and loop the straps over my shoulder. I'm ready with an excuse about why I'm bringing it with me, but Momma doesn't even notice, so I close the car door and head to the entrance.

The worker from the sign company is off the ladder. He has unhitched some of the letters and is now placing the *r*, *t*, and *i* in the back of his green pickup truck.

"Hello," I say. "What's going on?"

"New owners," he says. "Harnetiaux Pets is now Happy Pets. I'm updating the sign."

"Oh." I take one last look at Momma as I head inside, hoping she might have changed her mind. This is why I miss noticing that someone is kneeling low and polishing a stack of glass fish tanks.

Step-trip-clunk! I barely catch myself on the edge of a shelf.

"Whoa," the boy and I say at the same time. "Sorry."

He stands and brushes my shoeprint from his jeans.

"Are you okay?" I say. "I hope I didn't leave any permanent marks."

"It was my fault." He flicks black bangs from his eyes. "I'm good. You okay?"

"Uh-huh." We're face-to-face now, and I realize he is good, as in, really good to look at—kind, flirty eyes, and a perfect uneven smile. My cheeks warm.

"Sorry. I don't usually trip customers as they walk in the door." He sets a bottle of blue Windex on the counter. "Welcome to Happy Pets, or you can call us Li Pets, because I think we should copy Mr. Harne—"

"It's Happy Pets," a woman's voice calls from another aisle.

"Okay, Mom," he calls back, but then whispers to me, "Li Pets."

I smile and wonder why I've never seen him before. He looks like he's my age—I'm good at guessing these things—plus, we're practically the same height.

"As you heard," he jabs a thumb to the aisle behind us, "the boss likes Happy Pets better."

"Both have a nice ring," I say.

"Yeah," he says brightly. "I'm Justin. As in, Justin

Li of Li Pets. By the way, that's *L-i*, the Chinese spelling, not *L-e-e*. That would be the Korean spelling."

"Okay," I say. "I'll be sure to pronounce it with an *i*."

Justin laughs, and it's such a nice laugh, it makes me laugh back all loud and goofy.

"Exactly!" he says. "Because Li Pets—"

"Happy Pets," the woman's voice calls.

He rolls his eyes but grins, too. "Want a tour? We've rearranged a few things."

"Okay, thanks." His smile forms a small dimple in his left cheek. I wish I could think of something to make him laugh again. "I'm Sage." I leave out my last name because no use blowing a new friendship in case he's already heard of the Sassafras name.

We walk down the pet food aisle, and Justin talks about the organic brands and how dog food has different meat varieties and grain-free options. He points out the giant blue-and-silver bags and then the medium and smaller bags. He talks about the treats—Greenies for fresh breath, chicken chews for healthy joints, and every size bone you can imagine. His voice is smooth, and I can't make the cheeseball grin leave my face, which must look crazy, because who gets this happy about dog food? We stop near the end of the aisle by the collar-and-leash section.

"What kind of dog do you have?" Justin asks.

"I don't."

He laughs. "Why'd you let me go on and on about our dog foods?"

"I don't know. I didn't want to interrupt." I don't tell him that I like hearing him talk. I pick up a blue collar with sparkly stones around it. "When I get a dog, remind me to buy this one."

"Will do." Our eyes lock for a moment.

I fumble to return the collar to the shelf. "Um . . . where do you go to school?"

"We lived in Colorado Springs until my family bought this store. I've been homeschooled by my dad, and now I—"

"Excuse me," a bearded man in orange flip-flops says. "Where can I find the cat litter?"

"Just one aisle over on the right," Justin says. "Would you like me to walk you to it, sir?"

Please say no.

"No thanks. I'm good." The man heads off.

Phew.

Justin waves an arm to the left side of the store, where I can hear puppy barks and squeaky toys. "This way to the highlight of the store."

My smile grows. We walk to an open area, and Justin says, "This is where we've built out the puppy zone and rescue dog area."

"Holy magenta!"

"Yep," Justin says, smiling as he and I look at the new construction. The shelves that were here when it was Mr. Harnetiaux's store have been removed, and in their place is a waist-high plexiglass fence enclosure. Six full-grown dogs run around inside a large play area.

Justin takes a ball from his pocket and rolls it to a small pit bull the color of cinnamon and coral. "Here you go, Peaches." He checks the clock hanging on the store wall and says, "Right now, the rescue dogs get their playtime. Later, it will be puppy playtime. I'm still figuring out how to work the schedules."

"Whoa, you're in charge of that?"

"That's right." Justin stands a little taller and his sweet, uneven smile makes me stare a second too long. I tuck a loose strand of hair behind my ear, and suddenly, I'm wondering how my hair looks and wishing I were wearing my white jeans—minus the pickle stains—instead of a pair of old blue corduroys.

Five dogs run around one end of the enclosure, tossing balls and playing tug-of-war with a small purple rope. A white dog hangs out in the corner. Justin leans against the fence. "Watch this." He points to a cider-brown dog bouncing its way to the white dog.

The cider dog grabs the white dog's tail and tugs on it until the white dog barks and starts a game of chase. Justin laughs. "They do this all the time. Aren't they cute?"

"Mm-hmm." *And so are you.* I clear my throat. "People can just go in and pet them?"

"Yep. The dogs that aren't socialized yet stay in their cages and we work with them one-on-one. I like to make sure each dog is ready to live with a family."

"I love dogs, too," I say awkwardly. "I mean, I know you didn't just say that, but it's kind of obvious."

"We have two rescues at home," he says. "I want to make Peaches my third."

"I can't wait to have a rescue of my own." Maybe when the curse reverses that'll happen right away—a dog for Daddy and me and a guinea pig for Momma. "One day."

"And it'll wear that blue collar."

"Exactly!" I keep smiling and I'm not really sure what to do with my hands, and now I'm worrying he thinks I'm a complete weirdo to come to a pet store and talk about dogs when I don't even have one. "Um, I like looking around. You can't be too prepared."

"Good motto," he says. "When you settle on a pet, come back and see us. My mom is setting up her vet clinic back here." He points to a door. A stack of boxes and a pile of furniture still wrapped in plastic sits against the wall.

"I mean, I hope you'll come here a lot before you get a pet, too." Justin smiles down at his shoes.

The color that bumps around inside my chest is Snowy Soda's apricot-orange. It matches the happy-fizzy-awkward way I'm feeling now.

Neither of us say anything for a long moment, so I fill the silence: "So, um, your mom is a vet?"

"Yeah. And my dad runs the store. He's out buying more cleaning supplies like brooms and mops. Guess who's going to have to put those to use." He points two thumbs at his chest.

"You?"

Justin grins.

We lean over the fence to pet the dogs, and our arms graze. Bubbles fizz in my chest again. I'm having the best day ever, until I catch sight of Mrs. Snyder coming out of an aisle carrying dog food.

Mrs. Snyder stops at the endcap next to the pooper scoopers and narrows her eyes like she's warning me not to run over and steal her purse. I send mind waves back telling her I'm going to win the Noodler contest and become a world-famous artist, and she'll wish she had been nicer to me.

A short woman with shiny black hair and bright

white tennis shoes walks up to Mrs. Snyder. "May I help you with anything?" It's the same voice that spoke to Justin earlier—his mom.

Justin says something to me, so I turn back and he calls to Peaches, "Come here, girl. You'll like meeting Sage."

Apricot-orange still flickers in my heart; however, I feel a gray cloud edging close.

Justin stretches his hand into the play zone and scruffs Peaches on the head. She licks his fingers.

"Awww," I say, but I'm distracted. Mrs. Snyder is now in a full-blown conversation with Justin's mom. Doom snakes down my back. Nobody can have that many questions about pooper scoopers. Plus, the way Mrs. Snyder leans close to Justin's mom while glancing my way makes it clear what she's actually discussing— or more accurately, who.

Great, I think, and by "great," I mean green-guts horrible.

Then Mrs. Snyder lifts her nose in the air, and Dr. Li marches toward me. Justin turns to see what has my attention.

"Uh-oh," he says in a whisper, "here comes my mom, and by the look on her face I can tell I'm in trouble for something."

My stomach plummets. *I'm* the something.

"Hello," Dr. Li says, more suspicious than friendly.

"Hi." I sound like the guilty criminal she thinks I am.

"Mom," Justin says confidently, "meet Sage."

Dr. Li folds her arms across her chest. "Sage, our store policy is backpacks and grocery sacks are to be left up front."

I flush.

"Mom?" Justin says.

"We have a customer at the cash register, Justin," Dr. Li says. "Please go ring him up."

"Really? I love doing the register! BRB, Sage." He dashes off.

"Umm." I shift nervously. "That means 'be right back.'"

"Are you here to purchase something?"

"Ah, yeah, yes. Yes, ma'am. I'd like to buy crickets."

She eyeballs me. "Do you have a pet lizard or pet frog?"

"Um, frog." The lie sends heat up my neck, but she doesn't notice.

"Follow me." She walks to the reptile section full of large glass aquariums. One enclosure has lizards sitting on warming rocks, another has red-spotted frogs, and another has a leopard gecko. We stop at an aquarium that holds hundreds, maybe even a thousand zombie-gray crickets—enough to flip Priscilla's skin inside out if she were here.

"These are the crickets we recommend for feeding to frogs. It's two fifty for ten. Did you bring money with you?"

I swallow. "Yes, ma'am. I have ten dollars."

She's not even impressed, just gives me a blank stare.

"Um, may I have ten crickets, please?"

She snaps on plastic gloves and crinkles open a brown paper bag. She reaches her full arm into the cricket aquarium. I get the willies watching her pick up one twitchy body at a time, and I can almost see why Priscilla doesn't like these guys. Dr. Li seems pretty calm, though, and I wonder if it's because of her years as a vet. Does she pick up frogs and scorpions and snakes, too? Since we're not on a friendly basis, I don't ask.

When she's done, she closes the aquarium. Then she folds the bag shut and tosses the gloves into a trash can.

I reach for the bag, and she hesitates before handing it to me. "I'll walk you to the register."

Shame heats my face and burns inside my ears. *I've done nothing wrong,* I tell myself, and pull my shoulders out of their slump. I am not a street rat.

Nosy Mrs. Snyder watches me the whole time. She acts like she's inspecting the leopard gecko, but I know better.

I follow behind Dr. Li's bright white tennis shoes until we are next to Mrs. Snyder, and I can't help myself. I stop. "Look!" I say, crinkling the bag open under her chin. Crickets shuffle and chirp and one jumps toward her big nosy nostrils right before I snap the bag shut.

"Oh, my." Mrs. Snyder clutches her heart. "Oh my." The loose skin on her neck wobbles.

"In case you're wondering," I say sweetly, "I'm just buying something with the money I got legitimately for my birthday."

Dr. Li narrows her eyes, studying me. "Are you ready to pay now?"

I stand a little taller. "Yes. And I'm sure you're busy, so I can find my way to the register on my own." The crickets shuffle and chirp. Mrs. Snyder backs away.

"I'm sure you can." Dr. Li crosses her arms and continues waiting for me.

There's something on her face that I can't read until it occurs to me that how I just acted toward Mrs. Snyder has confirmed everything negative Dr. Li must be thinking about me.

My throat dries. My moment of pride comes to a

pathetic end. I lower my chin to my chest and follow Dr. Li to the register. I have no idea where Justin is, because I can't bring myself to look up. Dr. Li pokes a few air holes in the bag, and I use my ten dollars and the quarters to pay. She gives me an even eight dollars back. I drop the cricket bag into the Sprouts sack and rush out the door.

I'm across the parking lot when I hear, "Hey." It's Justin calling to me from the doorway. "Nice meeting you, Sage!"

I fake like I don't hear, because all I can think is how he'll change that tune just as soon as his mom gives him the lowdown on what Mrs. Snyder had to say about me, aka "Shady Sassafras."

The backs of my eyes burn and I fill with anger. Momma should've come into the store with me instead of making me face Mrs. Snyder by myself.

When I climb into the car, Momma's nose is buried in her book. I toss the Sprouts bag into the back seat and slam the door shut.

Momma startles. "Wha—"

"I'm done." I cross my arms.

"What's wrong?"

I can't tell her I bought crickets and how ugly that went. "Nothing," I say with crackling-red anger. "I just thought we were going to the pet store *together*. It would've been nice if you came in."

Momma spies Mrs. Snyder making her way to her car. "Did that Snyder woman say something to you?" Momma's voice crackles with red now, too. She unbuckles her seat belt. "That's it. She can taunt me, but I will not have her bullying my daughter."

Hearing her have my back cools my pulse. "It's okay."

But she opens her door. "No. It's not."

"Momma, please."

"No, I won't have her—"

"*Please!* I don't want a scene. I just want to go home." My voice breaks. "Please."

Momma hesitates before rebuckling her seat belt and closing the door. After a moment of quiet, she picks up the golden leaf still sitting between us and hands it to me. "Honey. I just want you to know we're from the same tree. We're in this together."

I grab for the leaf. Somehow, it's already dry, and it cracks, scattering pieces of Momma's offering on the car floor.

CHAPTER 14
SUNDAY, DECEMBER 16

On Sunday at noon, the phone rings at exactly twelve o'clock, just like it does every Sunday. Momma answers on the first ring.

"Hello," she says, all excited.

I pick up my sketchpad and pencils, walk to my room, and close the door. I lie on my paisley comforter and try to practice Noodler sketches, but the walls are thin and I hear murmurs of her conversation with Daddy. My shoulders tense. It'll be my turn to talk soon. My insides tangle—he might ask me if I read his letters or say something that I'm not ready to talk about.

I open my pad to a blank page and scratch the

Mars dust red pencil back and forth, coloring circles or hearts, I'm not sure. My stomach twists. What am I going to say?

Twelve minutes go by, and I've worn down the pencil tip. Daddy only gets fifteen minutes of phone time. Maybe Momma will use up the whole time, but I'm not sure I want that, either.

Knock, knock. Momma opens my door. My pencil freezes in my hand. My skin feels clammy.

"Honey," she says, holding out the phone.

My heart speeds, and I make my decision—I point to my throat and mouth, *sore throat.*

She shakes her head and soft-whispers, "That's what you said last week. Take it."

I put the phone to my ear and continue scribbling with the red pencil. "Hi."

"How's my favorite artist?" he says.

My heart clenches in a painful squeeze. There's that voice, warm and kind. The voice that read Harry Potter with me. The one that always knows—knew—just what to say.

I take a shaky breath. "Fine." I set the pencil down.

"Did you have a nice birthday?"

"Mm-hmm."

Momma stands in my doorway, nodding at me to say more. My mind goes blank. I take the phone away from my ear. "Please go." I wait for Momma to shut the door before I put the phone back to my ear.

"Sage? Sage?" he says.

"Yeah?"

"I hope you received my card."

"Yep."

"Did you and Bailee do something fun?"

"Mm-hmm."

"Like what?"

"Movies."

"Nice." I hear the strain of effort in his voice. "Which one?"

I know he wants more from me. But I guard each word, careful to make sure he doesn't hear my questioning. *"Star Wars."*

"Sage, I love you. Please talk to me."

Then another voice comes on, the automated recording. "This is the Federal Correctional Institution. Your time has expired." A click is followed by dead air.

"Don't worry, Daddy," I say now that he's no longer on the phone. "I have a magic candle, and as soon as the curse-reverse works, you'll be home, and we'll talk about everything."

CHAPTER 15
MONDAY, DECEMBER 17

On Monday morning, Momma goes into work extra early, and I wake up to practice Noodler logos before I have to leave for school.

After an hour of sketching, I grab my crickets and go to the kitchen. I slice a bright green Granny Smith apple for breakfast and pop a bite into my mouth. It's delicious, both sweet and sour. I put a slice aside for the crickets, so they can have a snack to munch on while they wait for my plan. The apple is the last of the fruit from the groceries, but I'm not worried—if I win the Noodler contest and become super-famous, people will probably send me big congratulations baskets full of creamy cheeses, sweet fruits, and salty crackers.

Plus, as soon as the curse reverses, we'll have tons of food. I lean against the kitchen counter and crunch into another apple slice.

Hmm, I think. My crickets need a safer way to ride to school in my backpack other than a squishy bag.

I go to the pantry and take some Bubble Wrap from one of the framed photos and loop it around the cricket bag, but the bubble wrap blocks the air holes, so I take it off. Next, I search my cabinets and find the turquoise plastic storage container we use for leftover soup. Momma's not going to like me ruining it, but I puncture the lid with a knife to make air holes.

I put the apple slice inside the container. Now I just need to move the crickets to their new home. I open the brown bag and peer down. Ten zombie-gray crickets crawl over one another. On Saturday, it seemed like a lot, but now it doesn't look like many at all. I dump the bag into the container.

Chirp! One jumps out and dashes away. I snap the lid closed so no more can escape, but now I only have nine crickets. The escapee hops under a space in between our cabinets. It feels like a bad omen and makes me worry my plan will be a dud. I should have spent all ten dollars on crickets so I could have four times as many.

I could use today's wish to have more crickets, though.

Why not? I've already made my important wishes—Momma will have money to pay bills, Daddy will come home soon, and the curse will turn in our favor. Everything else is icing, plus, I get a wish every day for the next five days.

I hesitate. Bailee won't like me wishing without her. But . . . she'd love seeing me win against Godzilla for once.

I set down the turquoise container, open the kitchen drawer, grab the magic candle, and light it. "I wish the crickets in this container would quadruple in number!"

Drip, drip, drip, drip, drip, drip, drip.

I blow out the melting candle but not before losing a quarter inch of wax. Now the candle is about the size of a piece of penne pasta, a little over an inch tall. Dang it. But this will be worth it.

My hands shake. It's freaky to think there might be forty crickets in my container now, or thirty-six if I'm being exact, but I don't really like exacts. I peel open the lid a tiny bit and hold my breath.

Nine crickets crawl around on top of each other. They chirp, and I swear they're telling me I'll have to be patient for this wish, too.

A cricket hops, and I snap the lid closed before there's another escapee. I return the candle to its fancy box and put everything back in the kitchen drawer. Part of me wants to tuck it away somewhere in my room, but there's no time for that right now.

I place the cricket container at the top of my backpack. Finally, Priscilla will get her payback. She gets everything great in the curse, but this time I'm coming out on top. After I lock up the apartment, I rush to the bus stop, energized to unleash the best plan since the invention of practical jokes. Godzilla will think twice before she pulls another trick on me—this is going to go down in the history books as the prank that ends all pranks!

CHAPTER 16

The bus is quiet. Most kids in Goldview aren't talkative on Monday mornings, and I wonder if it's like this all over the world. In the back of the bus, the eighth graders stare out the windows. In the row across from me, Steven sleeps and Hudson looks at his phone. Bailee is sitting beside me, reading *The Outsiders*. She turns a page and says, "Stop fidgeting."

"I want to talk about Minerva's."

"*Shhhhhh.*" Bailee has already shushed me twice, but I'm dying to tell her about the quadrupling wish and the mega prank. "Not here," she whispers.

"But—"

"*Shhhhhh.*"

I want to confess about using the candle without her, and I'm about to try again when she says, "There are too many big ears around here." She looks around the bus suspiciously.

"Okay?" I don't know who has big ears, but it's probably better this way. She might freak if she knew she was sitting next to nine crickets . . . or forty! But she's going to be impressed with how great this goes down. Maybe with my Noodler win *and* the prank I won't just become regular-famous. I'll be ultra-famous, and nobody will ever make fun of a Sassafras again.

Still, waiting in all this quiet makes me nervous that someone will notice my crickets and warn Priscilla before I have a chance to pull off my prank. Crickets mostly chirp at night to find a mate or to keep other male crickets away, but the turquoise container is dark, so they probably think it's midnight, and I swear I keep hearing them chirp. I make my own noise and shift in my squeaky vinyl seat.

Thankfully, the bus starts moving, the engine rumbles, and Mr. Melvin pumps tunes from his Motown Monday playlist.

"Turn it up," I call out, not only to mask cricket chirps, but also because Motown Mondays are almost as good as Funky Fridays.

When Mr. Melvin arrives at the next stop, he smiles

at me through the mirror and clicks up the volume by one notch. Then he cranks open the door and takes a sip from his steamy cup of Java Hut coffee, which, by the way, is twice as expensive as the café coffee, according to Momma. It smells rich and earthy, so maybe it's worth it.

"Are you okay?" Bailee asks. "Or are you trying to set a world record in fidgeting?"

"Haha." My laugh is awkward. "Can we please just go over everything again?"

She reluctantly closes her book and says, "If we are going to talk about you know what, let's keep it on the down-low. We don't want just anyone going to Minerva's for a magic candle."

We hunker low in our seat and whisper about the magic, going over the bazillionth rehash of what a curse-reverse will look like when it finally happens.

"My momma will stock Cherry Garcia ice cream in our freezer every weekend!"

"Check!" Bailee says.

"And we'll have yogurt parfaits for breakfast."

"Double check," Bailee says.

"And the jury will figure out they're wrong and send my daddy home."

"Um," Bailee says. "That's not really how the court system works."

"Well, somehow they'll let him come home."

"Okay." Bailee's voice falters. "Umm, check."

"And then Gigi will be our friend again."

"Why's that?" Bailee asks.

"Duhhh. All roads lead back to the curse. Why else do you think she stopped being our friend?"

Bailee shrugs. "Because she's interested in different things."

"No, it's the curse!" I clap. "Oh, and maybe we'll buy our old house back!"

The bus jolts over the railroad tracks and Steven groans.

Hudson, who is in the seat right beside us, asks, "What are you guys whispering about?"

Bailee and I giggle, and she gives me the leg-squeeze code of "we'll talk later."

Mr. Melvin stops the bus, and a bunch of elementary-grade kids load on and fall into seats.

"Are you guys whispering about the contest?" Hudson says. "Don't let Priscilla go scaring you out of entering, Sage. I need some real competition."

I smile.

"Also," he says, "I did some research, and come to find out, the majority of past winning entries came from artists who didn't use a lick of technology."

"True story?" I ask, sitting up.

"Yep." He takes his phone from his pocket and says, "Winners used watercolors, colored pencils, markers. Here, I'll show you." He types some words into his phone but I cut him off.

"Thanks, Hudson. You don't need to prove anything." I pause. "I'm not worried about Priscilla."

"Really?"

I nod, and Bailee says, "Sage's mom gave her colored pencils for her birthday. She can use those to make her entry."

"Or something else." I waggle my eyebrows.

"No! You can use the colored pencils." Bailee sounds super-bossy. "You'll participate fair and square."

"Ever heard of a joke, Bay?" I'd never want to win a contest by cheating.

More kids, all ages, load on, and Ryan and Curtis come down the aisle, take seats, and say hellos. Curtis plops in front of Bailee and me.

Chirp!

"What part are you on?" I say loudly to Bailee, tapping her book.

"When Ponyboy says that Robert Frost poem to Johnny. 'Nothing Gold Can Stay.'"

"Oh yeah," I say. "I had to read the poem twelve times to understand it." When I did, it made me think of my daddy. "It means nothing perfect can last. But the poem's wrong, because our friendship is perfect and it'll last forever."

"Yep." Bailee smiles. A moment passes and she adds, "I love that Ponyboy wants to recite the poem to Cherry. It's *sooooo* sweet." Bailee places her book over her heart. "Wouldn't it be great to have someone recite poetry to us?"

Curtis looks over his shoulder and smiles.

Chirp!

"Okay then!" I say loudly. "Any jokes today, Curtis?" We can always count on Curtis for something funny, and sure enough, he keeps us laughing for most of the ride.

My laughter stops when we pull up to the red light in front of Happy Pets. Justin is outside, sweeping the sidewalk. He looks up, and I have a flicker of hope that maybe his mother didn't say anything bad about me. I lift my hand and make a small wave, and just when I do he turns his back.

He saw me, right?

Of course he saw me. He probably heard an earful about my infamous father. A sinkhole of shame caves in my chest. *Welp*. I slouch and look away. Nothing gold can stay.

CHAPTER 17

As Bailee and I head to the bank of sixth-grade lockers, we pass sign after sign announcing "Four days until the solstice!"

Bailee and I have side-by-side lockers. The happy-birthday poster and photo she taped on the outside of my white metal door are still in place, but someone has drawn a mustache over my face. Godzilla stands just a few lockers over.

"Nice move, Zilla."

"You're welcome, Weed." She crosses her arms.

"Sorry," Bailee says to me. "I can make a copy of that for you."

"Thanks." I rip down the mustached photo.

Godzilla is about to get hers.

I twist my lock combo and I'm so distracted I mess it up.

I glance at my enemy again. Jada and Gigi gather around Priscilla, and honestly the three of them could be models for a hair commercial—Jada with her cool red-brown 'fro, Gigi and her glossy black side braid, and Priscilla and her sleek blond A-line cut.

Bailee nudges me. "What's up?"

I shrug. "Hair envy." This makes me think of how awful my hair looked when I met Justin. "Why don't we ever try different things with our hair?"

Bailee reaches into her locker. "I'm game. Like what?"

"I don't know." Bailee and I wear the same old ponytail every day. And the same outfits every week. Today, Priscilla has on a stylish Olympic-blue shirt with mid-length sleeves and a new pair of Converse Chuck Taylor high-tops. They must've been custom-made, because they have a picture of a boa constrictor on the side, maybe even her family's boa constrictor.

I spin my combination and this time the lock clicks open.

"I should sue the Xcel Energy Company," Priscilla says. "I still cannot believe our electricity went out right in the middle of my party." Her tone lightens.

"But perfect timing, since I was sitting next to Steven."

Jada and Gigi giggle. It's Gigi's real laugh and it makes me miss hanging out with her.

Priscilla grabs strawberry ChapStick from her locker and drops it into her backpack. "Have you ever heard of such a thing as an electric company shutting off someone's power?"

I expect Gigi to say something like, "Yep. Happens all the time at Sage's." Instead she says, "I can't believe they did that on your birthday party."

"Right?" Priscilla says. "Why in the world?"

"You think your parents forgot to pay the bill?" Gigi sounds like she's trying to help solve the mystery, but Priscilla blisters five shades of mad and pops her hands to her hips. "Is that supposed to be a joke, Gigi? You heard my mom call Xcel. They said they lost her payment." Priscilla turns her angry glare on me. "And what are you staring at, Weed?"

Whoops. I didn't realize I was gawking. But I can't help it—her electricity went out and mine powered up on the very same weekend!

"Watch out, girls," Godzilla says. "I think Carl Sassafras's kid is trying to catch our locker combos."

"What would I steal from you?" I say to Priscilla. "Your ugly forty-dollar shoes?"

"Umm," Jada says. "I need to run."

"Yeah, me too." Gigi zips her backpack closed. "Later." She leaves with Jada.

Priscilla slams her locker door. "For your information, Weed, these shoes cost ninety dollars. You would know that if you weren't so busy shopping at Goodwill."

Heads turn my way, and I feel my face flush.

"Come on." Bailee reaches into my locker and plops a pair of generic white tennis shoes into my arms. "We're going to be late for gym."

I follow Bailee down the hall with my fists clenched so tight my nails dig into my palms.

"Just take a breath," Bailee says, stopping at the water fountain. "Let's fill up our water bottles."

I grumble and untwist my cap. Godzilla will get her payback soon and then she'll know what public humiliation feels like.

"No pouting." Bailee elbows my side playfully. "You have too many things to be happy about to let Priscilla slither under your skin."

She's right. "I know."

We fill our bottles and head to the gym. Maybe I should tell Bailee about the crickets now, so she knows I don't plan on losing today.

"Hello?" Bailee says.

"Huh?"

"I just asked you what you're going to wish for next."

I laugh and say, "How about a head full of lice for Priscilla?"

"No! Please promise me you won't waste wishes on stuff like that."

"Haha." My laugh turns stiff. "Of course not." Bailee will forgive me for blowing a wish once she sees how great it works out. We walk around the corner and I ask, "You think it's too much to wish that the curse-reverse hurries?"

"It's probably already reversing," Bailee says. "Think about it—Priscilla's lights went out."

"Right!" I smile. We arrive to a full locker room, girls dressing for gym class.

Thinking about my prank makes my smile double in size. Curse or no curse, I'm going to come out on top, and for once Godzilla will know what it's like to be on the butt end of a joke.

CHAPTER 18

Coach pops her head into the locker room and blows her whistle. "Let's go, ladies. PE starts now."

Shanie, Janet, and Lily run out to the gym floor, leaving just Gigi and me.

Gigi and I are always the last ones ready. Back when we used to hang out, we would joke about our slowness and call ourselves the leisure llamas. We even swore we would make llama pajamas one day, the ultimate leisure wear! I'd draw the llamas, and she'd sew up the comfiest outfits ever.

Joking about being a slow-changer is way better than admitting what I really try to avoid: peeling off my clothing in front of everyone in the locker room. I tell Coach I'm modest, so she doesn't dock me points for running late, but truth is I can't deal with Priscilla making fun of my old underthings. It's not like my momma can afford to just drive to Denver, run into Walmart, and buy me new bras and panties all the time.

I've become pretty good at changing without anyone seeing. Today, I put on my PE uniform extra slowly, first the navy-blue shorts and then the white T-shirt.

Gigi laces up her tennis shoes.

After Coach leaves, I lean toward Gigi and say, "Attack of the leisure llamas." I laugh, but we both know it's not my real laugh. She doesn't laugh with me, and I'm not sure if I feel stupid or nervous.

Gigi clears her throat, and I fumble with my shoelaces. "Um. Tell Coach I have cramps. I'll be out in a minute."

"All right," Gigi says, and hurries out to the gym.

I'm alone. *It's now or never,* I tell myself.

I unzip my backpack and take out the plastic container. The crickets are mostly quiet, which worries me, so I lift the lid for a peek, panic, and snap it shut. I'm not normally grossed out by bugs, but watching them step over each other's faces gives me the shudders. I'm so nervous and shaky, I'm not sure if I saw nine or forty. I just want to get this over with.

Hardly anyone brings a lock to PE, probably because we only have five minutes to change and nobody wants to waste time fussing with a combination.

When I find Priscilla's locker, I take a breath, glancing left and right. My hands shake. I open the metal door and take out her new blue shirt. I unfold it. My heart speeds. I strain to hear if anyone might be coming. Coach's whistle blows; I can hear balls thumping in the far distance. *Can I really do this to Priscilla?* I clutch the turquoise container.

It's not Priscilla, it's Godzilla, I tell myself. *Remember the pickles.* She deserves to be humiliated, just like she always does to me. She'll see the crickets and explode in a full freak-out, and everyone will laugh because she'll look ridiculous screaming about tiny little crickets, and then I'll say, "Touché, Godzilla. Think carefully before you decide to pull another fast one on me." Then I'll take a bow for delivering the supreme payback.

With shaky hands, I dump the whole pile of crickets, we're talking bug on top of bug on top of bug, inside her shirt. I can't look. I know I'm not afraid of bugs, but I've never handled a pile of insects before. I hop from foot to foot. "Ew, ew, ew." My arms tremble.

I refold her cricket-filled shirt, shove it back inside her locker, and slam the door closed before a single bug can escape.

After one more twitchy-shiver, I let out a *pheeeeeeeeew*. This is going to be awesome! I bury the container in the trash can—because, let's face it, I'll never eat soup from it again—and I run out to the gym floor.

I line up next to Bailee and Shanie at the red free-throw line.

Coach folds her arms and glares at me.

"What is wrong with you today?" Bailee asks.

"Why?" My hands shake at my side.

"You're already sweating."

"Oh," I whisper. "Just excited about wishing and magic."

"Me too! I've been thinking about what you said on the bus about nothing gold can stay. I want you to wish that we're friends for life. It doesn't break the free will rule, since we both want that!"

"Deal!" I say, and watch Bailee shoot free throws.

"Even though I know we'll never need that wish." Bailee stops shooting and looks me in the eyes. "It's more like for insurance."

"Yeah," I tell her, but as I think about it, I'm sure there's no point in wasting the wax. We've been best friends since the minute we met.

Basketballs thump and roll by my feet. Most shooters miss the net, but not Priscilla. Like I said, she's a great basketball player. I watch her technique. She tosses swish after swish into the basket, her knees slightly bent and her fingers spread evenly on the ball.

She catches me watching, and I roll my eyes, pretending like I'm not impressed. And why should I be? With a curse-reverse, maybe I'll shoot even better today.

"This isn't spectator time, Sassafras," Coach hollers. "Take a shot."

She lobs an orange ball my way. I dribble a few times. This ball has a good bounce, not like one of the flat ones. I turn it in my hands and take a forward step, making sure my toes don't touch the red line. I dribble again, put a bend in my knees, aim at the basket, and shoot. *Swish*. It flies perfectly centered through the net without even touching the backboard or rim. *Easy*.

I scoop up a ball rolling by my feet and do it again. *Swish*.

"Wow, Sage!" Bailee says. "I don't think I've ever seen you nail two in a row." She tosses another ball to me. "Do it again."

I dribble. Shoot. *Swish*.

Shanie claps.

Bailee squeals. "Did you practice in your sleep?"

I laugh. I used to practice with my daddy. "It suddenly feels right."

"Again." Coach lobs another ball my way.

I catch it, aim, and shoot. *Swish.*

Bailee screams. "Nice!"

Girls stop shooting and watch. Coach has one ball in her hand and another propped on her hip. She tosses the first.

Swish.

And the second.

Swish.

I can't miss. Priscilla stops and watches.

Swish. Swish. Swish.

"It's like magic," someone says.

All attention is on me, until Priscilla starts shooting again. Brick. Brick. Brick.

She can't sink a single shot.

Coach blows her whistle. "Good job, Sassafras. Okay, girls, time for dribbling drills. Everyone grab a ball and head over to the cones."

Jada scoops up two balls and hands one to me. "Nice shooting."

"Thanks."

We head to the cones, girls surrounding me, patting my back. Bailee is laughing and saying, "Yep, that's my BFF." Even Gigi high-fives me and says, "Nice!"

Bailee wags her eyebrows at me and mouths, *curse-reverse*.

A single basketball bounces. I look over and Priscilla shoots another brick. Is that what I usually look like?

Bailee nudges me and whispers, "I know I wasn't a big curse believer before, but after the electricity and now this, I think the curse-reverse is really happening."

"Right?" She doesn't even know the half of it, because the prankster is about to become the prankee.

"You usually suck." Jada laughs. "Sorry, that sounded mean, but it's like you and Priscilla switched roles."

I smile, until a cold plunge of worry sinks in my stomach. If I'm taking Priscilla's basketball skills, what is she getting of mine?

CHAPTER 19

A single cricket jumps from Priscilla's locker. "Ahhhhgk!"

Priscilla's scream is only a tiny shock, until she unfolds her blue shirt and her terror notches up to horror-film level. "AHHHHHHKKKKKKKKKKKKKK!"

Girls in the locker room glance over, trying to figure out what's wrong.

Priscilla flings her shirt as high as she can. It flies into the air in a rainbow arc, crickets riding it like a magic carpet until dozens tumble off on both sides. It looks like the crickets more than quadrupled! Some fall from the flying shirt and land on heads and down bras. The room explodes in screams.

The blue shirt keeps flying like it's in slow motion, and the worst possible thing happens. It kerplops right next to Bailee. More crickets stream out. Bailee screams and soars up onto a bench, hugging her arms to her chest and shrieking, "Please, somebody! Do something!"

Zombie-gray crickets chirp and jump. There have to be more than forty of them, maybe more than a hundred! It's impossible to count, because they're zooming and zipping every which way. Some get squished under feet, some fall out of ponytails. Guts line the floor, and even my stomach gets queasy.

My best friend's face is full of terror, and immediately, umber shades of regret slink under my skin. Why didn't I realize Bailee would hate this prank?

I bat bugs away from her with my PE shirt. "I've got you, Bay."

Bailee cups her hands over her glasses, and I'm pretty sure she's crying.

The crickets have definitely multiplied. They jump everywhere—under the benches and inside shoes.

"Germs!" Bailee screeches. "Crickets carry germs." Her voice quivers at a level I've never heard before. She wrings her hands. I knew Bailee wasn't a fan of bugs, but I greatly underestimated her reaction. Suddenly, I feel like the world's biggest jerk. How could I forget to connect crickets with her dread of germs? I. Am. The. Worst. Friend. Ever.

Coach runs into the locker room, blowing her whistle to quiet us until she sees what's going on. The whistle falls from her mouth. "Oh . . . my . . ." She's speechless for a moment until, "The boys' room is empty. Grab your clothing and change over there."

Girls around me shake out their stuff. A cricket falls from Jada's hair and she screams, "Ewwwww-wwww!" Some girls are laughing, excited about the drama. Others, like Bailee, stand on the benches, paralyzed.

I catch Gigi staring at me. I look away.

Bailee trembles.

"It's going to be all right, Bay." I pick up her clothing and check through it, turning it inside out, checking hems, and pulling out pockets.

"Nothing." I hold everything high. "Your shirt and pants are clean. No crickets."

"You promise?"

"I swear."

I scoop up my stuff, too. "Come on. I'll piggyback you."

She climbs onto my back, and I run us to the boys' room and put her down in front of the sink. Bailee pumps soap into her palms and rubs it up her arms all the way to her shoulders. "Thank you, Sage. You're the best friend ever."

"Yeah." A flush crawls up my neck. I scrub my hands at the sink next to Bailee, avoiding my reflection in the long mirror, not wanting to see the guilt smeared all over my face.

Priscilla stands by Coach, crying.

You'd think I'd be happy about Priscilla's sobs, that I'd revel in them, but I don't. Nobody is laughing at her. A few other girls are crying, too. There's no "touché" ready on my lips. In fact, I feel small. Smaller than small. Whatever is tinier than a cricket's burp, subtract ten and that's how small I feel.

I remind myself that Priscilla never feels bad when she throws shade my way. She didn't feel bad when she doctored my butt with pickles or drew a mustache on my photo or when she dad-shamed me on the bus. But those reminders don't make me feel any better.

Coach pulls her phone away from her ear. "Nobody is answering," she says to Priscilla. "I've tried calling both of your parents."

"I . . ." Priscilla sniffs. "Bugs were all over my clothing. I can't put them back on." Her voice is a quiver. "It's too gross." Tears tumble down her face.

"It's warm enough to wear your PE uniform for the rest of the afternoon. Would you like to do that?"

Coach speaks in the softest voice I've ever heard her use.

"She can't," Bailee insists. "The crickets jumped over everything she's wearing. There's no telling what they could have left behind."

"They're just crickets," Coach says, sounding tired from the effort of being nice.

Washing her hands has recentered Bailee. She puts on her lawyer voice. "It's a well-known fact that crickets carry parasites and bacteria in their bodies, like *E. coli* and salmonella, to name a few."

Priscilla shivers.

Coach's face tightens, but she takes a breath and says, "I'll try your parents one more time."

While Coach dials, Bailee offers Priscilla a squirt from her keychain Purell. Priscilla accepts and scrubs it over her hands and arms, sniffling to hold back more tears.

"I'm so sorry that happened to you," Bailee says.

Priscilla darts an angry glare at me.

"Nope. No way." Bailee shakes her head hard. "Sage didn't do this. Not in a million years." Bailee's certainty makes me wish it were true. She sets an arm around my shoulders and tells Priscilla, "I know you guys have your curse-feud, but Sage would never do anything with crickets, because she knows how much

I hate bugs." She looks me square in the face and smiles. "Right?"

I turn my back and change shirts. "That's right." My voice tightens. "Never." She doesn't see my eye twitch.

"I can't reach your parents," Coach tells Priscilla. "Come along. We'll find something in the office for you to wear."

Priscilla has to borrow something from the "ugly clothes" bin, just like she wanted me to do on Friday when she ruined my white jeans. For the briefest moment I feel satisfied. Until I look back at Bailee.

"Thank you so much, Sage," Bailee says with a shudder. "That was awful."

I put my arm around Bailee's shoulders and walk her back to the sinks. "Let's wash our hands one more time." I turn on the water.

She gives me a quivering smile. "You're such a great friend."

My smile quivers, too. She can never know I was the one who did this.

CHAPTER 20

By lunchtime, the cricket saga has grown, and all I can do is pray Bailee doesn't figure out I'm the evil villain in the story.

We are seated at the end of the bench at the same long table as Jada, Gigi, and a bunch of others, and guess who's right next to us—Priscilla! Bailee feels sorry for her and wants to make sure she's okay, and I'm too guilt-ridden to argue.

"Nobody has ever seen so many bugs." Jada's arms fling this way and that as she tells the cricket drama to the crowd of boys. "There were hundreds of crickets and grasshoppers and ladybugs flying everywhere."

Gigi nods, and the boys say, "*Ooooooooh.*"

Bailee says something to Priscilla and offers her more keychain Purell.

Priscilla takes some and smooths it over her hands.

"You'll probably want to use a Clorox wipe on your phone and the table, too." Bailee hands over a wipe.

"Thanks."

All the niceties between my BFF and my archenemy twist the nerves in my stomach, but maybe if Bailee stays focused on helping Priscilla, she won't stop to think about who's to blame for the prank.

Priscilla sponges down her cell phone, sets it on the cleaned table, and opens her copy of *The Outsiders*. "This book is actually really good," she says to me. "I need to catch up to the rest of the class."

"Oh . . . kay?" Peculiar, because reading is exactly what I would do if I were her.

Jada stands, pounding her hands on the tabletop. "There were too many to count!" When Jada tells a story, she's all in. She's the best in our class at theater. Her eyes grow round, like she's seeing it all again. "You could barely see the floor, there were so many bugs."

"Cool!" Ryan leans in. "And then what?"

Curtis bites into his ham sandwich and glances my way, and I'm paranoid that he's giving me some sort of look. Could he have heard something on the bus?

"And then Gigi . . ." Jada pauses dramatically as only people who are onstage do.

Gigi's eyebrows pop up. Her grilled cheese is already wedged in her mouth, so she crunches into its buttery-gold crust and nods as if she knows what Jada is about to say, even though none of us who were actually there know what Jada will say next.

"Yeah?" Steven says, his eyes wide.

Jada sets a hand on Gigi's shoulder. "Well, Gigi, who had already changed into her regular clothing, used her PE shorts to *bat* the bugs away." Jada begins miming like she's a bug-batting matador and hollers, *"Olé! Olé! Olé!"*

Hudson, Steven, and Ryan eat it up, laughing with each *olé*.

Gigi finishes chewing her sandwich, and a smile spreads across her face.

Jada adds, "It was Gigi who cleared a path for the rest of us to run to the boys' side before the spiders—"

"¡Ay, bendito!" Steven says. "There were spiders, too!"

"Yes! And other creatures, but since I'm not a bugologist—"

"Bugologist!" Gigi laughs. "You mean entomologist?"

Jada beams. "Thank you. Yes. Since I'm not an

entomologist, I can't name every insect we saw, but let's just say it was a regular bug version of *Jurassic Park*."

"Whoa," Ryan says to Gigi. "You're like an action hero!"

Gigi glows. She's had a crush on Ryan since fourth grade. At least I think she still likes Ryan.

Priscilla stares down at her book like she's unaware of all the *oooohs* and *ahhhs*. Super strange. The normal Priscilla would have planted herself next to Jada and taken over by now, but she stays seated at the end of the lunch table and turns another page. Maybe she's embarrassed about her clothing from the ugly bin. Instead of her cute jeans and new blue shirt, she's dressed in gray sweatpants paired with a slouchy tan top.

But here's the thing—I don't think she cares! Maybe because she's traumatized, or maybe because she's reading and lost in a story while I sit here worrying my best friend might discover I'm the worst person ever.

After Jada finishes her version of what happened, Steven informs everyone that crickets can tell you the temperature outside. "Yep," he says. "Just count how many times they chirp in fourteen seconds, add forty, and that's the temperature."

"Dude, you should be president of the science club," Ryan says.

Curtis marches to our end of the table and says, "Curious how so many crickets showed up out of nowhere." He's speaking to all of us, but I swear he's looking right at me.

My throat dries. "Yeah, curious."

He squats down beside Priscilla and Bailee. "Are you guys okay?" Curtis is not only funny, but he's also one of the nicest kids in Goldview.

Priscilla lifts her chin from her book. "Huh?"

"You okay?"

She takes a breath. "I'm good now. Thanks." Her phone chimes, and she reads the screen.

"How about you, Bailee?" Curtis asks.

Bailee grimaces. "I can't even talk about it."

"Hey, my mom just texted me," Priscilla says. "She's picking me up so I can shower and change at home. Do you want to call your parents, Bailee? We can give you a ride."

Huh? Does Priscilla think they're besties now? I don't think—

"Yes, please!" Bailee says. Zero hesitation.

What?

"Here." Priscilla passes her phone to Bailee.

I spend a moment lifting my jaw off the table

until—*Clang! Clang! Clang!*

"Students!" says Mrs. Downy. She bangs a metal spoon against a pan. *Clang! Clang!* "Attention, students."

The cafeteria quiets.

Mrs. Downy steps to the center of the room. "As most of you have heard, there was a cricket incident in the locker room during gym class today. Now, there are many conspiracy theories circulating around the school about where these crickets came from."

"Cricket-gate," Jada whispers dramatically, forgetting that Mrs. Downy has bat-like hearing.

"That's right, Jada," Mrs. Downy says with a *clang*. "Cricket-gate. Let's be clear. I will not be blamed nor have my standing as a JOTY contender put in jeopardy."

Curtis raises his hand. "What is *joty*?"

"Janitor of the year." Mrs. Downy points the metal spoon at her row of JOTY plaques hanging on the wall. Her eyes glisten. "I have won JOTY four years in a row, and now those janitors in Denver think they're going to take it from me.

"No!" She bangs the pot for emphasis. "I will not be blamed for this fiasco!" *Bang!* "I will not have our school's cleanliness questioned, and I will not be accused of doing a poor job as your janitor, so let's get to the bottom of this right now."

I swallow down a gulp the size of a storm cloud.

"Who brought . . ." She scans the cafeteria crowd.

I sit on my trembling hands. I made a huge mistake, and if anyone finds out it was me, I'll need to win a hundred Noodler contests to fix my infamous reputation.

"Who brought," she repeats, "food into the locker room?"

Everything is quiet except for the pounding in my ears. Then a small boy sitting at the table for first graders bursts out crying. "I'm sorry, Mrs. D.," he says with a lisp. "I ate a Fig Newton in there. I won't do it again."

I feel sick.

"Thank you for your honesty, Ahmed," Mrs. Downy says, "but this is not your fault. The outbreak began on the girls' side, and one cookie one time would not cause a problem of this magnitude. There are hundreds of crickets."

Hundreds? Did my quadrupling wish keep going hour after hour? Like did 10 go to 40 and then 40 to 160?

My panic rises.

Bailee nudges me and whispers, "What's wrong?"

I shake my head. "Nothing." My eye twitches.

"I know, bugs. Gross." She shivers. "You need some Purell? Do you want me to break out the pink pomegranate?"

"Um, thanks."

She pulls out her special pomegranate gel, the gel for special circumstances and emergencies only. I rub it into my palms, and I watch a first-grade teacher kneel beside Ahmed and dry his tears. Tears I caused.

"I will get to the bottom of who caused Cricketgate." Mrs. Downy scans the crowd again and my pulse quickens.

"Furthermore, Principal Bateman has informed us we will do without free frozen yogurt for a month, since we now need to pay Goldview Pest Control to handle the problem."

An eruption of moans and complaints explodes around me.

The guilt is crushing. I wish I had the guts to confess like Ahmed did, but I have too much to lose. I'm trying to stay calm by convincing myself no one will ever find out it was me, until I see him . . .

Justin Li!

I had assumed he was going to continue with homeschooling. But *noooo*. He's enrolled at Goldview K–8, and he's sitting on the far side of the cafeteria at one of the tables full of seventh-grade boys. My heart falls to my shoes—he knows about me *and* he probably knows about my cricket purchase. What's worse—I'm pretty sure he just gave me the stink eye.

In this moment, I'd trade all my remaining wishes to have my daddy pick me up from school the way Priscilla's mom is coming for her. Daddy is who I'd confess to. I'd tell him everything the second I saw him. He'd drive us to Sonic, and we'd order lemon-lime slushes, and he'd help me figure out how to fix Cricket-gate.

See, Momma is great fun when it comes to singing and laughing, but it's Daddy who knows how to listen. It was Daddy who used to answer my questions and understood when I was sad or mad or embarrassed. If he were here right now, I'd tell him about the pickles, the cricket fiasco, and Justin.

A Sunday call doesn't have space for all that. I don't have time to tell him about the Noodler contest and how bad I want to win to fix the Sassafras name. I don't have time to tell him about Momma's tears or about Gigi dropping me or about Godzilla. I don't have time to ask him what if Bailee and Momma find out I'm the worst person ever for bringing crickets to school? I don't have anyone to help me with the colossal mess I've created. Thinking about it drops a boulder-sized lump in my throat, and I sniffle back some tears.

And oh, sepia! If 160 crickets quadruple, it's going

to add up to 640 . . . and then to more than 2,500, and then to over 10,000, and then 40,000! What if the quadrupling never stops!

That's when I know what I need to do.

I need to make a visit to Minerva's.

CHAPTER 21

Bye, Mr. Melvin." I climb off the bus and convince myself that I'm not sneaking to Minerva's. That I'm going alone because Bailee went home after lunch, and I can't call her to meet me here since I don't have a phone.

Cars roll by. A cool, light breeze blows across my face. I rush past the graffitied walls and barred windows. At the city bus stop, I cross the street to the lavender building with the Hansel-and-Gretel red door.

Just as I get there, Minerva steps out of the store with a huge purse on her shoulder, holding the largest key I've ever seen. The key is shiny and black and has a lavender silk ribbon looped through the end.

"Well, hello again!" She sings her greeting. "Don't tell me you're here for another candle. You can't get greedy. It's one per customer, you know." Her eyes shine.

"No. I'm here to ask more questions about the magic."

"*Shh shh shh shh shhhhhhhhhh.*" Minerva looks side to side.

"Umm, sorry," I whisper.

"Just kidding!" Minerva laughs and slaps the side of her leg. "I'm practicing my joking skills. Pretty good, huh?" The red-raspberry leaves on the maple tree rustle and a dozen or so float to the sidewalk.

"Uhhh?"

"Come in, come in." She drops the key into her purse and opens the door. "Quickly, though. I have just a few minutes before I need to dash."

We go inside, and the lights automatically turn on their warm golden glow. The store smells of vanilla spice, and once again a feeling of enchantment glides across my skin. Minerva sets her bag on the counter and sweeps her long red hair from her shoulders to her back. "What brings you in today?"

"I'm here because I need to . . . to unwish a wish."

"Oh my!" Minerva takes hold of my wrist and checks my pulse: "Seven, eight, nine." She releases my arm and leans close, inspecting my eyes. "Please don't tell me you wished you could fly." She places a hand on my forehead. "That would take quite a few lessons, plus there's rumors about an incident in 1973 when a boy who received a candle—"

"No," I say. "I wished to quadruple the number of crickets I brought to school."

"Mm-hmm." Minerva folds her hands together. "And?"

"Well . . ." I stare at the "Be Kind" button pinned to Minerva's collar. "Um, I would like the quadrupling to stop."

"To stop? Did you not designate an end? Quadruple one time or quadruple until noon? Please tell me you designated an end time for the wish."

"No." I gulp. "I didn't."

"Oh dear. Ohdearohdearohdear!" Minerva walks round and round in a circle. "At least you said quadruple the number; the magic could have quadrupled their size. That could have been a disaster. But still, what shall we do? What shall we do? I thought you understood the rules."

My shoulders sink lower. "I know I'm not allowed to unwish a wish, and since I've already used up my one wish today I can't wish for an end time." My voice goes up a notch. "This definitely can't wait until tomorrow, otherwise our school will turn into Cricketville! Will you please help?"

Minerva pulls a stethoscope from under her shirt, plugs the ear tips inside each of her ears, and plops the cold round listening part against my forehead. "*Shhh*, for real this time." And then, "I see. I see," Minerva says to herself. She listens again and then wraps the stethoscope over her shoulders.

"Are you able to fix this?" I squeeze my interlaced fingers.

Minerva sighs. "I suppose we don't want Goldview to turn into Cricketview, so I will handle what must be done."

I exhale. "Thank you! Thank you so much!"

Minerva laughs. "As you know with the rules, you have no unwishing powers." She winks. "But I do. That said, unwishing magic is not free." Minerva reaches into the pocket of her long purple skirt.

"Oh?"

She pulls out her hand and flickers silver glitter over my head. The lights in the store twinkle.

Phst. I spit out bits that land on my lips and teeth. "Sorry." I swipe a hand across my mouth.

"Voilà," Minerva says, brushing her hands clean. "All better."

"That's it?" I ask. "The crickets are gone?"

"That's it." Minerva walks behind the counter and fumbles with a few things.

"Really? Now what? What do you mean by 'not free'?"

"Ah, here it is." Minerva plops a thick ledger on the countertop, and a cloud of dust rises. She opens the ledger's yellow pages to a spot marked by a lavender ribbon. "Where's your friend who pays attention to rules?"

"She had to go home early." I tell her about what happened at school.

"Ahhh." Minerva removes a purple feathered pen from her purse. "Sounds like you were a lousy friend. I trust you will fix that." Her voice is not judgy, but friendly as always.

I nod.

In fancy cursive, Minerva writes my name on the center of a page.

"What's that for?"

"The update," Minerva says in a singsongy voice. "We need to add an amendment."

"To what?"

"Well." She waves the feather at my nose. "You needed to cancel a wish, so I did, which naturally costs you a future birthday wish."

"A future wish? I thought the magic candle only worked until the solstice."

"Oh, silly! Everyone still gets to send up one wish on their other birthdays, with or without an enchanted candle. I mean, there's no guarantee it will work without the magic candle, but it's always worth a try. Now which birthday wish would you like to forfeit in this exchange?"

"Um . . . my seventieth?" *No biggie*, I think.

"Done." She jots something in the ledger and closes it. Dust or sparks puff from its pages. "Excellent." Minerva slings her giant purse over a shoulder and walks to the door. "Oh, I almost forgot to mention the tax. You've also forfeited half your remaining candle wax in this exchange."

"Half the wax!"

"Absotively. Now remember, you only have until sunset on the solstice, and then you know what happens."

"What? No, I don't know what happens!" It's the second time she's mentioned it. "What exactly does that mean?"

"It means wish wisely, silly!" Minerva grabs the doorknob. "Like they say in country songs, 'get 'er done.'" She giggles. "And do it before your generational chance passes."

She's so confusing. "You mean when the candle is done and the wishes run out, right?"

"Oh, goodness." Her eyes twinkle. "It's certainly not as simple as that."

"But—"

"Come, come. I have places to be and people to go." She swings open the door and ushers me outside. A bicycle skids to a stop in front of us.

It's Justin.

Justin, who gave me the stink eye. Justin, whose mom thinks I'm a criminal. Justin, who probably knows I purchased crickets at Happy Pets, and now he's followed me here to hold me accountable. It's *that* Justin.

And now there's no getting around the fact that I'm going down for this mess.

CHAPTER 22

Justin unlatches his helmet. "Hey."

"Hey." I step back, nervous, confused, and ashamed all at once. "Are you spying on me?" My voice shakes.

"Uh . . . no?" Justin says, lifting his helmet off his head.

Minerva smiles, and in her singsongy voice says, "It sounds like you two have a lot to discuss, so ta-ta." She locks the door and drops the giant black key into her bag. "Have a sparkly evening."

"Wait," I say to her back, "the solstice is four days away. What happens?"

She skips down the sidewalk.

"I still have questions," I holler. In fact, I have two burning questions: What's going to happen by the solstice, and how much longer will I have to wait for the curse-reverse to be complete so my daddy can come home?

"You'll figure everything out," she calls over a shoulder. "Be kind!"

What if I don't figure anything out, though? I watch Minerva until she disappears around the corner.

"Is she a doctor?" Justin asks. He's off his bike with his helmet looped on a handlebar. "Or a veterinarian like my mom? I only ask because of the stethoscope."

I shake my head. "What are you doing here?"

"Why?" He sweeps a look around. "What's wrong with here?"

"I don't like being spied on."

"Why would I spy on you?" He gives me his lop-sided grin. "Are you a secret agent or something?"

He sounds flirty, but I know better. He didn't wave back when I waved at him from the bus—probably because he knows I'm the daughter of a convicted bank robber. I cross my arms over my chest. "Seriously, why are you here?"

"Uhhh, because I'm riding my bike. Or is that a crime in Goldview?"

"Haha, 'crime,' I get it." I shoot him my best mean glare.

Justin smiles like I'm joking, but when I don't smile back, he looks confused. "My mom said I could go exploring. Check out the town."

"How is your mom?" I drag out the word "mom," and my tone screams attitude.

"Ohhhh." Justin's gaze drops to his neon bike pedals. "I'm sorry about that."

Good. At least he's not going to pretend she didn't say anything. "You don't have to believe everything you hear about me, you know."

"I know that," Justin says. "Geez. Is that what you think? I thought we were chill."

"Really? Then why did you give me the stink eye in the cafeteria?"

"In the cafeteria?" Justin thinks for a moment. "Were you there when that janitor lady did all the pot banging?"

"Uh, yeah, and then you gave me that mean look from across the room."

"Nope. Not possible," Justin says. "I'm nearsighted."

I uncross my arms. "You didn't see me in the cafeteria?"

"No. If I did, I would have said hi. I mean, I know you don't owe me anything, but it would've been nice for you to say hi to me on my first day of school."

He waits, and I don't say anything because my brain is trying to shift gears.

"Okay. Obviously, you don't want to be friends because of my mom." He sets his helmet back on his head. "I'm sorry for the way she treated you, but I'm not responsible for her behavior." He clicks the chin-strap closed and climbs onto his bike.

My head spins with what he said: he is not responsible for the way his mom acts.

Justin pedals forward and then pedals some more, and before he's too far, I holler, "Wait!"

His brakes squeak and his tires scrape to a stop. I run to catch up, and when I reach him, he gives me his lopsided smile and says, "Took you long enough."

My heart glows poppy-red happy. "I'm sorry. I just . . ."

"Just what?" Justin says, his voice kind. "You just assumed that me and my mom are the same person. Do I look like I wear her bright white tennis shoes? No. I love my mom. She's a great mom to me. But some-times . . ." He shakes his head. "Sometimes she can be embarrassing."

"Tell me about it. I mean . . ." I swallow. A gush of shame warms my face and my tone goes super-awkward. "Ugh, parents, right?"

Justin looks at his shoelaces. "Yeah." He grinds his toe into the sidewalk, and I can tell he's been told about Carl Sassafras.

My arms automatically cross over my chest. "Just so you know, my daddy didn't do it. The jury got it wrong."

Justin looks up and all easy-peasy he says, "Okay."

That's it. He's taking me at my word. The walls around my heart melt, and I uncross my arms. "You're not worried I'm going to shoplift at your store, or steal your lunch money, or do something villainous?"

"Why would I think that?"

"Some people around town think since my daddy is a felon that I'm one, too."

"That's dumb." He shakes his head. "My motto: 'We are not bellhops. It's not our job to carry our family's baggage.'"

I laugh and we start walking. "I wish everyone thought that way. I've had friends dump me because of my daddy."

"That's not fair," Justin says. "Nobody should be able to give you a reputation—good or bad. That's on you and your actions alone."

I nod.

"Let's agree that we won't hold our families against each other."

"Deal!"

"*Phew.*" Justin wipes his forehead. "And can we shake on it before you meet my brother? He's in college, and he's pretty mortifying."

I laugh again.

We cross the street. "So . . ." Justin clears his throat. "The crickets you bought at Happy Pets. I suppose you're behind Cricket-gate, huh?"

My shoulders tighten. I'm about to repeat the lie I told his mom about having a pet frog, but the honesty feels too good to mess up. I nod. "I feel terrible. Please don't tell anybody."

He does a zipping-his-lips motion and pushes his bike as he walks me home. It's nice talking to him, confessing to someone about the crickets, and taking a break from worrying about magic and curses. I tell him about Bailee and the Noodler contest and say, "Once I win the contest, I'm going to be world famous!"

"Maybe you need to give me your autograph now."

I laugh and ask Justin about his first day at Goldview. He says he liked it, that the Lab Rats seem like a fun group, and that he wants to go out for the track team.

The sun inches down farther, still warming my face. A few honey-gold leaves shake loose from the trees and crunch under our feet. We talk about how much I'd love to own a dog and how he has a pet bird he's training to talk. He says he thinks owning a pet pig would be the coolest thing in the world but he hasn't convinced his parents yet.

"A pig!" I say. "That's weird."

He laughs. "Pigs are actually smarter than dogs."

The sun starts disappearing behind the mountains in the west. "It'll be dark soon." I point at the headlight attached to his handlebars. "I hope that thing works."

He clicks it on and off. "Yep."

We arrive at the green spruces that line the parking lot outside my apartment building. A light breeze fills the air with pine.

"Four days until the solstice," I say, and stop walking.

"Yeah. Goldview K–8 really nerds out about the countdown," he says. "I love it!"

"Yeah," I say, wondering again about Minerva's words: *If you don't do what needs to be done before the solstice, you'll have to wait another generation.* I kick a pinecone.

"Does everyone go to that dance with friends," Justin says, "or do I need to ask somebody?" He smiles down at his bike pedals.

"Everyone just goes to it." Then I realize why he's

asking, and I smile. "You should come with me and Bailee."

"All right, I'm in!" he says.

I could float off the ground right now. And to think I used to yawn through Gigi's chatter about crushes. Now I get it. I have all the feels, which in today's color-speak is not only fizzy apricot but also helium peach.

Gravel pops behind us. We turn to see a purple helmet and a rider wearing reflective elbow and knee pads.

It's Bailee. And there's no time for me to tell Justin to keep it a secret that he saw me come out of Minerva's.

CHAPTER 23

Bailee looks so much happier than she did when she left school. Her cheeks are pink from riding, and she takes a breath, stopping beside us.

"Hi!" she says, giving me a who's-he look.

"Hey!"

"Remind me to never go home early again. My little brothers drove me crazy." She turns to Justin. "Hey."

"Bay, this is Justin. Justin, meet Bailee."

"Bailee the BFF?"

"Yep." She climbs off her bike. "Sounds like you know me, but I don't know you."

My stomach flutters—I couldn't tell her I met a cute boy when I went shopping for crickets. "Oh, um, haha, this is Justin from Harnetiaux Pets." Ugh, I've already said too much.

"Li Pets," Justin says.

"Actually, Happy Pets, hahaha." My laugh sounds so awkward it's embarrassing. "His family owns the store now."

"Oh." Bailee looks confused but happy. "And you guys decided to hang out after school?" She gives me the quickest eyebrow wag.

"Not exactly." Justin laughs. "Apparently Sage hated me after lunch for an alleged dirty look, but we're cool now." He smiles, and my cheeks warm. "Luckily, we ran into each other outside that purple store, so we could straighten out the misunderstanding."

Oh no.

"Reeeeeally?" Bailee narrows her eyes, telling me she knows exactly what store he's talking about even though he said purple instead of lavender.

"Alrighty!" I clap my hands. "You better ride home now, Justin. It'll be dark soon. Tell Peaches hello for me next time you're in the store."

"Will do." He snaps his helmet in place. "What about you, Bailee?"

She takes her helmet off and adjusts her glasses. "I'm staying. My dad'll pick me up later and throw my bike in the back of his truck."

"Okay, nice meeting you." He turns and gives me that perfect lopsided adorable grin. "Good hanging with you, Sage. See you at school tomorrow." He clicks on his headlight and rides off.

Bailee crosses her arms. "Well?"

"He's nice, right?" My voice quivers.

"You know what I'm asking." Bailee says this like she's cross-examining a witness. "The 'purple' store." She does air quotes.

"Ummm. Come on, I'll explain." I take hold of Bailee's handlebars and roll the bike across the parking lot, my steps slightly ahead of hers so she can't see if my eye twitches. "Yes, I went to Minerva's on my own. I . . . um, wanted to ask more questions."

"Like what?"

"Like . . ." And then I think up the perfect half lie. "I wanted to see if Minerva could help with the school's cricket problem, or if I could wish for that on my own." I ramble on, "I had to ask, because I wasn't sure if that messed with the free-will rule. You know, the crickets' free will." This is sounding dumber and dumber by the minute. "Anyhow, Minerva said she'd fix the problem because there could be too many possible complications if I tried to wish the bugs away on my own."

Bailee stops walking. "Sage!"

My heart freezes.

"That's the sweetest thing ever. Thank you so much."

Guilt. Guilt. Guilt. "Um, sure."

We carry Bailee's bike up the stairs to my apartment, me holding the front and Bailee lifting the back end. At my door, we lean it against the wall, and Bailee says, "Maybe today's wish can be the one about us being forever friends."

I gulp. "Listen. About that." I lift my silver key from the chain around my neck and rub my fingers over the notches. My ponytail falls forward and I hope it hides my face. "Um, Minerva said since she had to use her own magic to help with the school bug problem, I, umm . . . I used up today's wish." I turn my back to Bailee and slide the key into the metal lock.

"Sage! You're the best friend in the world! You knew I'd be too scared to step foot in that locker room again, so you traded your wish for me!"

I'm super-close to confessing that I'm the biggest lying jerk on the planet, but something feels wrong when I twist the key. "Hold on." I turn the knob. "The door is already unlocked?"

"Hello," Momma calls from inside.

I swing open the door, and there sits Momma at

our little dining table with bills, envelopes, stamps, and her checkbook neatly lined up under the flickering yellow light of a slender green candle. My magic candle!

"Blue bunny rabbits, Momma! What are you doing?"

"Getting organized." Momma stays hunched over the papers in front of her. "The electric company said my check bounced, so they turned off the power again." She shuffles the papers around. "I can't for the life of me understand how I let our finances get so out of control."

I stand there stunned, staring in disbelief at my twelfth candle propped inside a small glass jar. Pebbles at the bottom hold it in place. It burns a bright yellow glow, and a single bead of wax drips down its side. Layer upon layer of melted green wax coats the pebbles below. The candle is about three-quarters of an inch tall—reduced by half—and I know I've just paid Minerva's price for unwishing magic.

Bailee nudges me. "Hurry."

I drop my backpack, rush over, and snatch the candle from the jar. I take a breath to blow it out, but Bailee slaps her hand over my mouth.

"What in the world?" Momma says, stretching back in her chair. "Don't take the candle, Sage. I need the light." And here's the thing—Momma doesn't say this sweetly. She stands up and as Bailee backs away, Momma scrunches her face, picks up the end of my ponytail, and sandpaper-whispers, "And what is going on with your hair? It's a mess."

I stagger.

Momma drops my tangled ponytail and heads to the bathroom.

Bailee tugs me toward the kitchen and speed-whispers, "Remember the rule? You have to make a wish before the candle is blown out or else you deactivate the magic for good."

A drip of wax warms my fingertips, magic wasting away. "I don't have a wish left today, Bailee. Remember how Minerva handled the crickets? We need to find a loophole before I blow it out!"

"Okay, um, let me think." Bailee pauses. "Got it. Say you're making the wish for tomorrow." She squeezes my arm. "Hurry."

My guilt about lying to Bailee and about dumping crickets in Priscilla's shirt, her cute new shirt, makes me rush and say the first thing that pops into my head. "My tomorrow wish is that Bailee and I get new clothing."

Drip, drip, drip, drip, drip.

Candlelight dances across Bailee's unhappy-looking face. "Blow it out!" she screams.

I blow it out, and the candle shrinks to a nub shorter than my thumbnail.

"All that wax!" Bailee says.

"I know."

Chirp! The room is shadowy, but we still see the zombie-gray cricket, the morning escapee, jump by our toes.

Bailee screams and my nerves are shot. I join her for a double dose of *"Ahhhhhhhhhhk!"*

Momma walks over to the bug and—

STOMP!

She murders it!

"Stop screaming!" she snaps, and then rubs her temples.

Bailee hugs my arm. I'm pretty sure my jaw unhinges. I hide the candle behind my back.

"It's just a bug!" Momma rips a paper towel off the roll, squats by the dead cricket, and wipes its guts from the floor. "Where's that candle, Sage?" she says in the sternest voice I've ever heard my momma use. "I can't pay bills in the dark."

"I'll . . . I'll find something better for you, Momma." I whip a look at Bailee, and her eyes are as round as basketballs. Is she thinking what I'm thinking—that this curse-reverse is turning ugly?

Momma tosses the paper towel into the trash can and washes her hands. I use that moment to hide the magic candle in the deepest, darkest part of the mess drawer and set other birthday candles on the counter. I need to get Bailee out of here so we can talk. "We'll be right back, Momma. We'll run next door and borrow a flashlight from Miss Tammy."

"That's a great idea." Momma takes a breath. "In fact, we'll all go to Tammy's." Her normal sweet tone is back. "I'm sorry, girls. The bills have me stressed out." She sighs again. "I'll gather my papers and meet you there."

"It's okay, Momma." I rush Bailee out the door and grab her arm. "My momma killed a bug!" I whisper-shout. "Probably the first in her life!"

"I saw!" Bailee throws a hand on top of mine and squeezes.

"And she sounds like Mrs. Petty!"

"I heard." Bailee frowns and says, "So . . . about the wish. Um . . . thanks? But I thought you were going to make the friends-forever wish we talked about."

"I know. I couldn't think straight. I'll wish that next." I turn away and knock on Miss Tammy's door before Bailee can press the issue.

It swings open. "Lil' Spice and Bay Leaf!" Miss Tammy says. Motown music, the kind Mr. Melvin loves, plays from the speakers. She dances as she says, "Come in, come in."

"Electricity is out again," I say. "Momma will be over in a minute." The smell of lasagna wafts from the kitchen, and naturally my stomach does a monstrous growl.

"Goodness!" Miss Tammy laughs. "It sounds like I'm having company for dinner! You girls like Italian, right?"

"Yes!" we say. "We'll set the table," I add.

"Perfect." She shuts the door, and we follow Miss Tammy to the kitchen. "You know where everything is. I need to check the oven."

The music changes and now a jazz song pumps from the speakers.

"*Mmmm-mm*. It doesn't get better than B. B. King," Miss Tammy says, setting the timer on her stove.

I take out four blue-checkered placemats. Bailee grabs the red dishes.

We set them on the glass table, and I whisper to Bailee, "What am I going to do about Momma?"

Bailee shakes her head, darting a look at Miss Tammy. "We'll talk later."

We get silverware, and I tell Miss Tammy all about the Noodler contest and how I'm going to be famous and how Bailee will handle all my legal affairs. Miss

Tammy chops lettuce and tosses it into a big glass salad bowl. She cuts up cucumbers and olives, too, and we each pop a salty olive into our mouths. Then Bailee pours four glasses of water, and I set out white paper napkins.

Momma walks in the door without knocking. She's holding the phone to her ear with one hand and a bunch of bills in the other.

"How much?" she says into the phone, her voice high and jittery. She listens for a moment and then drops everything. The phone bangs to the ground and tumbles under a chair. The papers and envelopes flutter to her feet.

Momma's face turns ashen.

"What's wrong?" I bend down and fish for the phone. "What is it, Momma?"

Miss Tammy places a gentle hand on Momma's arm, and Bailee gathers up the papers.

"That . . . that's Re-Bay." Momma points to her phone, which is now in my hand.

"Okay?"

"Talk to them!"

I hold the phone to my ear. "Hello?"

"Are you there, ma'am?"

"Yes," I say, but Momma starts talking again so I tell the Re-Bay person, "Just a minute, please."

Momma keeps pointing at the phone, her hand trembling. "One . . . of the frames your father bought from a yard sale." Her voice catches. "One of those frames . . ."

"Uh-huh?"

Miss Tammy puts an arm around Momma's shoulders. "Here, sweetie, sit." She helps Momma to a chair. "Slow down. What is it you're trying to say?"

"One of those frames has a piece of art in it worth a lot of money, and a collector has submitted funds to purchase it." She puts two hands over her heart and takes a big breath. "Re-Bay wants to know where they should wire the money."

A man's voice on the other side of the phone says, "Hello? Hello?"

I speak to him. "How much money did you say it would be, sir?"

"One million two and some change," he says.

"A million dollars?" I look right at Bailee, and I can tell she's thinking what I'm thinking—my money wish from Friday is complete! "We're rich!"

I squeal. Bailee squeals. We jump up and down and in a circle. Now the magic just needs time to finish cooking the curse-reverse. Big changes are coming! I squeal again.

Momma grabs the sides of her head and shouts like

I've never heard her shout before. "Quiet!"

"Rosemary?" Miss Tammy says to Momma, looking shocked.

Bailee and I stop our celebration; my insides turn cold. Big changes are coming, but I'm no longer sure that's a good thing.

CHAPTER 24
TUESDAY, DECEMBER 18

The next morning, Momma is home when I wake up. She's back to sounding sweet and says, "We are taking a personal day and going shopping in Denver!"

"Whoa, shopping on a Tuesday?" A zing of lemonade yellow soars through my veins. "I guess that's what millionaires do!"

Momma laughs. She calls school and work and tells them we're not coming in. She makes a few more calls, and I spend the time practicing Noodler sketches for the contest. Being rich won't change the gossipers; they'll probably think we stole this money. I still need to win my fame.

But something's wrong with my art today. All my drawings keep ending up in a peculiar slant, full-on crooked, or with odd proportions. And the colors are all wrong.

At nine thirty, Momma says, "Ready?" I close my pad, and we head to the car.

Once inside, I buckle my seat belt. Momma starts the engine, and it makes its normal clunking sounds.

"Cherry Creek Mall, here we come." I can practically hear what she's thinking—*Hooray, Denver, where nobody knows our infamy.*

"How much gas do we have?" I ask.

"Full tank."

"Really?" The mall is about forty-five minutes away. I lean over to check the dashboard. Sure enough, the gauge is on full.

Momma gives me a sideways look. "I can take care of us, Sage."

I twist my mouth. *Maybe.*

We pull down the road with the radio playing. A Mimi Glosser song comes on, and we sing loud and off-key, laughing the whole time. I settle in my seat, feeling safe and happy and thinking the curse-reverse is going to be all right.

Several gold, orange, and red-raspberry leaves cling to trees; others have fallen to the sidewalks and flutter as we drive past. It's easy to figure out when we've left Goldview, because the temperature plummets and the autumn colors disappear into brilliant white snow.

"*Brrrrr,*" I say.

Momma clicks on the heater, but it doesn't work. "New clothing today," she says. "New car next week!"

At Cherry Creek Mall, we park in Nordstrom's covered lot and rush from the cold to the heated indoors. It's warm and cheerful inside with festive music and sparkly lights.

I stop walking. "Wait, Momma. I have to see it all." I crane my neck to look at the holiday decorations on the ceilings and archways and then all around the store. Nordstrom's managers must have hired a theater crew to build their huge winter wonderland scenes—green-and-white snowcapped trees, giant silver balls, and woodland animals. They also have a miniature lake that looks real with frosted blue ice and skaters. It makes me smile thinking of how Daddy, Momma, and I used to go ice skating.

"It's lovely," Momma says, rubbing the cold from her hands. "Come on, this way." She directs me to the café. "Let's grab a couple of warm drinks."

Nordstrom Café is bright, and holiday music flows from the speakers. The chalkboard menu is looped with greenery and on the top sits a bird's nest strung with pearls and silky blue ribbons.

One customer stands in line ahead of us. I check out the glass case filled with cranberry muffins, banana bread, and oatmeal cookies. Then I see the yogurt parfaits. My stomach growls, but I'm not about to ask Momma for one—they cost twelve dollars each!

When it's our turn, Momma orders lemon ginseng tea, and she's given a special honey stick to melt into it. I order Daddy's favorite, a hot chocolate. The barista towers it high with fluffy whipped cream.

"Thank you!" I say.

"We'll have a couple of yogurt parfaits, too," Momma says as she winks at me.

My feet float off the ground. I can't help but think it's the Pettys' breakfast, and that the curse-reverse is taking hold and all is well!

Momma uses her credit card to pay, the same card she used to have the electricity turned back on at home. For a fleeting moment, I hold my breath, wondering if it will be declined, but the charge goes through just fine.

We sit at a café table and chat about all the stores we want to visit and the things we plan to buy. When we finish our drinks and parfaits, Momma says, "Let's look at shoes first."

The mall has two floors and probably over one

hundred stores. There are restaurants and coffee shops and even people who will show you how to do your hair.

We shop for hours and buy a new purse and cashmere gloves for Momma, and shirts, sweaters, skirts, pants, and underthings for me. My favorite purchase is a pair of purple Converse Chuck Taylor All Stars. And Momma doesn't even blink when I ask her to buy an outfit and shoes for Bailee, too. She's generous that way.

After we eat turkey-and-cheese paninis for lunch, we pass a store that sells just pajamas. Right in the big glass window is a long-sleeved powder-blue cotton top with a llama on it. Llama pajamas! "Momma! I need those pj's!"

"You've got it." We go inside the store and find the right size for me.

We wait in line and when it's our turn, Momma slides her credit card into the chip reader and smiles at me. "This day reminds me of my first Christmas with your daddy. He bought matching red-plaid pajamas for him and me." She has a faraway smile. "We stayed in them all day long—breakfast, lunch, and dinner."

"Aww."

"Please sign," the tired-looking cashier says.

Momma removes her credit card and signs. "He

gave me a guinea pig pup, too."

"Really?" I can't keep the startle from my voice—I thought guinea pigs were a taboo subject around Momma. "I never knew you owned another pet after the boa constrictor incident."

The cashier gives me a funny look.

Momma's face changes. I've said the wrong thing.

"Here you go." The cashier hands the bag to me and calls, "Next."

Holiday music keeps playing, and I wait for Momma to say something. I follow her out of the store and into the busyness of the mall, people rushing this way and that. I try again. "Um, what color was it? Your guinea pig?"

Momma stops walking and fiddles with her wedding band, her thoughts far away. Shoppers step around us. I stay still, not wanting to make another wrong move, hoping to stay inside this rare moment. Momma lifts her chin. "Your daddy gave me a light brown one," she says, smiling. "I know you must think it's weird, Sage, my reaction to guinea pigs."

"Well . . . I'm sure it was hard, seeing . . ."

Momma puts an arm around my waist and we walk slowly. "Snowball was the name of my pup when I was your age. He was tiny and white and fit right into the palm of my hand."

I blink. She's really talking to me. Really opening up.

"The hardest part about the snake incident wasn't watching Candice Petty's snake swallow Snowball. It was that Candice gave him to me and said we'd be friends forever. And I believed her, but then the lightning and the curse, and . . . you know the rest. I lost so much all at once."

"I'm sorry, Momma."

"It's okay. That was a long time ago."

Momma starts to drop her arm from my waist, but I grab her hand and keep it in place. "Tell me about the guinea pig Daddy gave you? Where did you keep it? Did Daddy surprise you or did you pick it out together?"

Momma laughs. "It was a surprise." Her phone rings. "Give me a minute." We sit on a granite bench and she takes her phone from her new leather purse. "It's Miss Tammy," she whispers to me. Then back into the phone, "Hi, Tammy! Sage and I are having a great time." Pause. "Oh, sure, like a three-way call? Yep, I'll hold." She winks at me.

It's nice to put the bags down and sit. I rub my arms.

"Hi," Momma says brightly to whoever is the third party on their conference call. "Yes, very exciting." Pause. "An accountant? Not yet. Mm-hmm. Right. The taxes? How do . . . ?" She listens, her face tenses. "To be Carl's new lawyer?" The call goes on like that for another ten minutes, Momma's face turning more and more strained.

I smile at her, but she stares off in the distance.

"Is that possible?" she says into the phone. "How . . ." Pause. "Okay, thanks, you guys. It's all a bit much to take in at once. Can we talk later?"

Momma rises from the bench, rubbing the sides of her head. "I feel a headache coming on."

"But you were telling me—"

"Not now—"

I'm desperate to hold on to the connection we were building. "But what happened to the guinea pig Daddy gave you?"

"Nothing stays forever, Sage." Her voice is sharp, and I gasp.

"He died when you were a baby." Momma must see the shock on my face, because she softens. "Sorry, honey." She rubs her temples. "My head is really throbbing."

That's it. No more conversation. We take our bags out to the car and drive in silence. After we drop off Bailee's outfit, we go home. Momma heads straight up to our apartment. I grab the mail. Inside, I put the bills on the table and stuff another letter from my daddy into my top drawer.

That night, I shower, wash my hair, and go to bed in my soft cotton llama pajamas, feeling like the little princess from that book by Frances Hodgson Burnett. I even try to pretend my daddy is off to war. Only problem is tonight I can't pretend all those unopened letters stuffed in my drawer are from a hero on the battlefront and not from prison. Tonight, everything feels a little too real for make-believe.

CHAPTER 25
WEDNESDAY, DECEMBER 19

O n Wednesday morning, I wake clenching my teeth: the solstice is two days away, and I only have two wishes left—one on Thursday and one on Friday. I'm starting to wonder if I should be patient and trust the curse-reverse or if I should just wish Daddy out of jail. Added to that, I still don't understand what Minerva wants me to wish for by sunset on the solstice. A pebble of worry starts knocking around my rib cage.

On a positive note, my new-clothing wish has come true thanks to the shopping spree. My closet is packed with a dozen new things to wear. I push aside my covers and bounce out of bed—should I wear the green shirt with the jean skirt, or the soft gray sweater and blue jeans, or maybe the blue-striped shirt and the red skirt? I pull my white jeans out of my closet and toss them on the floor—good riddance, pickle-stained pants. I run a hand over the hangers of new clothing and choose the red skirt. I finish slipping it on when Momma says from behind me, "Hey."

I jump. "You're not at work!"

"Nope, I called in again." Momma sips her honey-and-lemon-scented tea. "I'm not sure if that skirt is right for you after all."

"It's not?"

Momma looks me up and down. "The salesgirl at Nordstrom looked cute in it, but . . ." Momma scrunches her face and stares at my waist. "Maybe we should have picked up a bigger size."

My excitement fizzles. "Oh." I put a hand over my stomach.

"Here." Momma grabs a pair of jeans with a special wash and a purple mid-sleeve shirt cut in the latest fashion. "This will look great." She sniffs. "Make sure you put on deodorant before you get dressed."

She walks out of my room, and calls back, "I do hope you'll do something with that hair of yours."

The color that pops to mind is scaly green, because Momma probably doesn't mean to, but she's making me feel small like Godzilla does.

I go into the bathroom and use lavender-scented deodorant, slip on the new outfit, and brush my hair five different ways. Forget it—I pull my hair into its regular ponytail and return to my bedroom. I stand in front of the full-length mirror hanging on my door. For a quick second, I think I look amazing. Daddy would say so. But Momma's words linger, so I shift and check again. Am I pudgy? Do I stink? Is my hair okay? Does everything fit? I gulp—my purple shirt is exactly the same as the new blue shirt Priscilla wore on Monday! The shirt I sabotaged with bugs.

I tear it off and change into a soft, cream-colored sweater. I lace up my new Converse, wondering if Priscilla's mother spends mornings saying the same confidence-shattering things I heard from my momma. Maybe that's why she shows up to school with so much mean in her.

I hurry to the kitchen.

The curse-reverse isn't 100 percent complete, because the refrigerator is still empty. The pantry is mostly empty, too. I grab the lone can of Pringles and shove it in my backpack next to my sketch pad. Ugh, I should have practiced Noodler sketches this morning instead of wasting so much time on my hair.

I swing by Momma's room, hoping now that I'm

dressed and combed, she'll say something sweet. "Bye, Momma. Love you!" I shuffle from foot to foot, waiting for her to notice me.

She looks up from the papers spread across her soft beige bedspread. "Have a good day."

That's it.

"Umm, you too." I race out the door, my stomach grumbling and my mind worrying while I jog to the bus stop. Momma's not acting right. As much as I want to believe a curse-reverse is going to be all good, I'm growing more and more worried it's not.

When I climb on the bus, I'm huffing from my run and fall into the seat with Bailee, our usual spot, nine rows down to the right, me by the window and her by the aisle. Bailee is wearing the same old clothes she always wears instead of the new outfit Momma and I bought for her. "Why'd you wear that" flies out of my mouth, my tone snotty.

"Because I like my clothes," Bailee snaps.

"Right," I say. "Sorry." I shudder at how I sounded. Like Godzilla. Like Momma. "Rough morning."

"It's all right," she says. "Honestly, I just wasn't ready to wear that new stuff. I appreciate it, but it felt super off having your mom carry a new outfit into my house. When you ran back to the car to grab the shoes, your mom wasn't herself."

"Oh no." I cringe, thinking how rude she's already been to me. "What did she say?"

"She said, and I quote, '*Now* you can dress for success,' and she said it like what I own is too shabby for words. You should have seen the look on my parents' faces. Anyhow, I thought it would insult them to wear the new stuff today."

I look around to see if anyone's listening before I whisper, "It's weird, but my momma is acting harsh . . . like Mrs. Petty. I think I messed up by wishing for a curse-reverse."

"Yeah." Bailee pulls me low in our seat. "I've been trying to think of what we should do."

"I sort of want to unwish the curse-reverse?"

"You can't. That'll deactivate the candle," Bailee whispers. "And Minerva said unwishing wouldn't work."

"It wouldn't hurt to at least try," I say. "I'm desperate here."

"But what if it does hurt?" Bailee leans closer to me. "What if deactivating the candle takes away the magic you've already received? Your mom will lose all that money."

"Sepia! Everything we bought yesterday went on her credit card! There's no way she can deal with more bills without the Re-Bay money." I think for a few moments and say, "Maybe I could wish for Momma to be nicer—"

"I thought of that, too," Bailee says. "But it breaks the free-will rule."

I think of how Minerva handled the quadrupling wish and say, "Maybe Minerva can fix the wish for me."

The bus hits a bump, making us wobble.

"Yeah," Bailee whispers. "It's worth asking."

"We should also ask what she meant when she said . . ." I pause and change my voice to imitate Minerva's singsongy tone, "'If you don't do what needs to be done before the solstice, you'll have to wait another generation.'"

"Right!" Bailee says. "I can't figure that one out."

"I feel like there's so much we don't know." I pull my sketch pad from my backpack and open it to the page with my last drawing. "I'm scared the curse-reverse is affecting more than just my mom. Look, my latest Noodler sketch sucks." I hand the pad to Bailee and hope she'll tell me it's not as bad as I think, and that I still have a shot to go from infamous to famous.

She tilts her head and shifts the pad this way and that. Her mouth curls down. "Not your best work."

I slide even lower in my seat and put my pad away.

"Sorry," she says. A blast of cool air pours through the windows.

Mr. Melvin takes a sip from his Java Hut cup, turns up the music, and says, "B. B. King. *Mmmm-mm.*" He shakes his head side to side, and the way he says it reminds me of Miss Tammy loving B. B. King, but it also reminds me of how Daddy used to say my name when he'd say, "Sage Sassafras, *mmmm-mm*, you are one great artist."

Not anymore. I bite at my nails.

"*Mmmm-mm*," Mr. Melvin goes on. "Greatest blues musician of the twenty-first century."

Steven hands his weather marvel book to Hudson and stands to push his window closed. Gold leaves flutter by. "Quick Flores Report," he says. "Weather is changing."

"Yep," Hudson says. "Winter's coming."

"Hey, Hud." I stop biting my thumbnail. "How's it going with your logo for the Noodler contest?"

"Pretty good." His eyes spark and he talks fast. "Mr. Lehman is going to let me use his acrylic paints! I'm going to practice with the cheap paints I have at home, and when I'm ready Mr. Lehman said I could use the good stuff in the library. How about you?"

I shake my head. "I've got zip."

"Come on. You're lying. You better be. Priscilla is going to give us a good run this time."

"Huh?" The tendons in my neck tighten.

"Yep, she showed me. Her art is looking pretty dang good."

I turn to Bailee and panic-whisper, "Sepia! I took

basketball, and Priscilla got art. My chance at fame might be kaput because of the curse-reverse!"

"*Shhhh.*" Bailee looks side to side. "Like you said, back to you-know-where straight after school." She takes out her copy of *The Outsiders*, opens it up, and ends our conversation.

All I can do is crack my knuckles and pray Minerva doesn't out my quadrupling-bug wish to Bailee.

CHAPTER 26

The bus makes a *pump-hiss* sound as we make the next stop. Elementary kids load up in the front seats and wave out the windows to their mommas. The last kid to climb up the steps is the small first grader from Monday, Ahmed, the one who cried because of me and Cricket-gate.

A fresh wave of ocean-blue guilt floods me.

Ahmed scoots into his seat and presses his hands and forehead against the window, peering at the crowd of parents.

"Mama," he calls as loud as he can. "I forgot my snack!"

I search the gathered parents. There's no way

his mother hears him over the rumbling of the bus engine. The bus bounces forward, parents wave, and Ahmed sinks into his seat.

A little way down the road, Mr. Melvin stops to pick up Ryan and Curtis.

We start moving again, a full bus—Hudson scrolling through his phone, Bailee and Steven reading, Gigi twirling her hair, Curtis and Ryan probably dreaming up jokes or thinking about Lab Rats and the solstice dance, elementary kids probably wondering what's for snack, and Mr. Melvin humming his music. Maybe this is the family I should draw for the Noodler logo— my Goldview K-8 family. The idea makes me smile until I remember I might've lost my art skills.

Curtis shifts around to face Bailee and me. "You ready for my latest joke?"

Bailee sets down her book and beams. "Give us your best!"

"The world-champion tongue twister just got arrested," Curtis says. "I hear they gave him a real tough sentence."

Bailee and I laugh.

Curtis says, "I was writing a song about tortillas, but it turned into more of a wrap."

"Haha." I chuckle. Bailee looks confused and Curtis's face falls a little. I elbow Bailee. "You know, because *r-a-p* and *w-r-a-p*."

"Oh, haha."

"Okay, not your favorite," Curtis says. "I'll keep thinking." Instead of turning around, though, he clears his throat and rubs the back of his neck. "Um," he says quietly. "I have something else."

"Another joke?" Bailee asks.

"No, um . . . something different." Curtis's voice shakes. He takes a breath. "I'm going to say it before I chicken out." His tone turns softer than soft, like he doesn't want anybody else to hear. He looks right at Bailee and says,

Nature's first green is gold,
her hardest hue to hold.
Her early leaf's a flower;
but only so an hour.
Then leaf subsides to leaf.
So Eden sank to grief,
so dawn goes down to day.
Nothing gold can stay.

"Huh?" I say.

"Ponyboy," Bailee says softly, holding up *The Outsiders.* "From our book."

"I know. We just talked about it the other day."

I sound like a know-it-all, but I can't seem to stop myself. "The poem Ponyboy says to Johnny and wants to recite to Cherry."

The bus engine rumbles.

Curtis focuses on his thumb, running it across the dull metal bar on the top of his seat. "Yeah," he says. "The poem he got from Robert Frost."

I've never heard Curtis sound so awkward.

"What do you think?" he asks Bailee.

"I don't get it," I say. "Why are you learning it?"

Curtis shrugs.

"You nailed it," Bailee says, her eyes shiny.

Curtis bites his lower lip, holding back a smile. "You think?"

"Whoa," I say, too loudly. "Are you doing this for a girl?"

Hudson and Steven glance up. Steven says, "Who do you like?"

"Is it Jada?" I ask.

"No." Curtis laughs nervously. "Why would it be Jada?"

"Because she loves theater, and you love performing. Duhhhhhh."

Bailee elbows me. "Sage. Do you even hear how rude you sound?"

But my mouth won't stop running as I'm figuring

things out. "Wait, did you say that for Bailee, because she said she loved how Ponyboy wanted to say it to Cherry? Are you going to dye your hair blond, too, like you're her Ponyboy?" My laugh sounds mocking and it's finally at this moment when my scaly-green tone settles on my ears. Ryan, Steven, and Hudson are staring at me like I'm a beast.

Because I am one.

I have turned into Godzilla!

"Está bien rara hoy," Steven whispers to Ryan.

I don't know what that means, but I wouldn't blame Steven if he just called me a monster.

Curtis faces forward and sinks low in his seat.

"I'm sorry, Curtis. I don't know what's wrong with me."

He doesn't say anything.

Bailee scoops up her backpack and moves to sit beside him. "I loved it, Curtis." Her words come out as soft as feathers. "Even better than your jokes."

"Really?" he says.

I strain to hear.

"Yep," she says. "Would you by chance want to go to the solstice dance with me?"

I lean forward. "That's great, you guys."

"Please don't talk to us right now, Sage," Bailee says.

My shoulders sag. My best friend is sitting in front of me, lining up a date, her first date, and I can't be part of it.

The curse-reverse is ruining everything.

CHAPTER 27

The bus pulls up the circle drive at school.

I stay seated and let Bailee leave the bus without me.

"Bye, Mr. Melvin." I climb down the steps behind the last eighth grader.

"You cheer up, now, okay?" Mr. Melvin says.

"Thanks." I run inside to catch up to Ahmed and find him outside one of the first-grade classrooms. "Hey."

He looks up at me, question marks in his eyes.

I hand him my can of Pringles. "For snack time." I don't stay to see if he even likes Pringles, and my guilt about him doesn't go away, but it's the least I can do.

It's lonely to walk in the hallways without Bailee. White paper signs that say "Two days until the solstice!" line the walls. Minerva's comment about once in a generation comes back to mind. What the heck does that mean? I stop at the water fountain. A solstice poster flutters down next to my new purple shoes. I step over it. Another countdown sign is taped to my locker, like someone is warning me. Minerva wants me to do something by sunset on Friday. But what?

I see Bailee down the hall and run and catch up to her. "I didn't mean to be a jerk. Can we be okay now?"

She looks forward as we walk. "It would be best for our friendship if I take a quick time-out from you, especially with the curse-reverse in action and not knowing what's going to happen next. Let's just take a break today."

"A break until the end of the day?" I whine.

"At least until lunchtime." Her tone is serious.

We both have PE now, but instead of making our way there together, Bailee rushes ahead, leaving me feeling blizzard white. Alone.

"Hey," Gigi says, walking up beside me. "Were you sick yesterday?"

I look around to make sure she's talking to me before I say, "No. I spent the day with my momma."

"Did you hear they closed the gym for the day?"

"Uh-uh." I shake my head.

"Yeah. Mrs. Downy found a hole in the locker room where she thinks the crickets snuck in from the outside. I guess it's all fixed now."

"Oh."

Outside the gym entrance, Mrs. Downy stands in her regular crisp tan pants and navy-blue shirt. She makes us form a line so she can inspect our bags for food. Priscilla and Bailee line up together; Gigi's behind them, and then me. Fluorescent lights shine and buzz overhead.

"The gym is a cricket-free zone," Mrs. Downy tells girls as they move forward and show their bags. "And a food-free zone. I will not be robbed of the JOTY."

Bailee inches forward with Godzilla, and I can't believe my eyes—she's offering to share her pink pomegranate hand gel, as in, the special-occasion gel!

I never thought I'd get jealous over sanitizer, but my stomach sinks. I stare at the globs in their palms. It's like Priscilla is stepping into my shoes, and she and Bailee are suddenly BFFs!

That worry pebble knocks against my ribs again, telling me I should've wished to be friends forever with Bailee like she wanted. Now it might be too late.

"I'm super-nervous about seeing the gym," Priscilla says to Bailee. She rubs her hands together, spreading around the pomegranate scent like a big fat show-off.

"Nothing to be nervous about," Mrs. Downy says, inspecting their open backpacks.

Surely, Bailee is going to turn and offer some pomegranate gel to me, too. I arrange my face in a smile to show that I'm okay with her helping Priscilla. I can be a big person.

When Mrs. Downy finishes her inspection, Bailee drops the gel into her backpack, loops her arm through Godzilla's, and pulls her toward the locker room. "We'll check it out together." Arm in arm, they head inside.

A cold frost fills my chest, making it hard to breathe.

"Hey," Gigi says to me. "You good?" She flashes a look at the doorway Bailee and Priscilla disappeared through and then back to me.

"Um, yeah."

Gigi hands her bag to Mrs. Downy and waits while my bag is checked.

We walk to the locker room together. "How did you figure out your baller skills?" Gigi asks.

All you need is a magic candle and a life-ruining wish, I think.

I shrug. "I just made a tweak here and there."

We go down an aisle of lockers and she drops

her stuff on a bench. "You mind showing me those tweaks?"

"Um, sure." I look for Bailee across the locker room. She has her arm looped in Godzilla's. They squeeze close, elbow to elbow, walking around inspecting every inch and aisle of the perfectly clean space.

Gigi is still talking to me. ". . . and I'd really love for you to teach me how to land a shot so the ball never touches the rim." She pulls her shiny black hair into a ponytail.

"Uh-huh. Sure." I turn and call over to Bailee and Priscilla, "*Helloooo,* you guys. Mrs. Downy said all the crickets are gone."

They stay in their own little conversation, ignoring me.

Blizzard white.

I'm wearing new underthings from my shopping spree, so I change into my PE uniform along with everyone else. I lace up my shoes and head into the gym. I'm not sure who to hang out with, until Gigi jogs up behind me and says, "You promised to give me pointers."

I smile and line up with her and Jada. Gigi snags a couple of balls and tosses one to me.

"Um, stand like this," I say, mimicking how I saw Priscilla setting up the other day. Then I think of instructions my daddy gave me when he'd try to show me his baller skills. "Soften through your knees, spread your fingers wide under the ball, and keep your eye on the hoop." I shoot and the ball swishes in the net.

Gigi gives it a go but misses. Jada's ball hits the backboard.

"That was really close," I say.

We do it again, and the third time both Gigi and Jada land their shots. The three of us high-five. I shoot a few more swishes, and Jada does a funny sports announcer's voice: "Ladies and gentlemen, Shooting-Star Sage Sassafras can't miss." We bust out laughing. I look for Bailee, wishing she were laughing with us, but she's been keeping her back to me the whole class.

We gather more balls. Gigi continues asking me questions, but I'm distracted. I can't help but worry I traded my art skills for hoops. I try sending mind waves to Bailee, dying to talk to her about it, about anything, but she won't make eye contact. She really isn't going to talk to me until lunchtime. When Bailee makes a rule, she sticks with it.

During science, I can't talk to Bailee since I have Miss Clonts and she and Priscilla have Mrs. Churnside. I spend the period doodling a cartoon of Godzilla.

It ends up looking like a first grader's salamander.

After class, I pass Justin by the water fountain. "Hey, Sage!" He gives me that awesome lopsided grin before rushing toward the seventh-grade hallway. It's like spotting a rainbow in the middle of a storm—red, orange, and yellow dance over me. I wave hello and try to hold on to the colors, but the second he disappears in the crowd, a gray cloud moves in and I'm back to worrying about Bailee.

I get to math class before Bailee and sit in my regular spot. The room smells like the chicken noodle soup steaming from Mrs. Floss's green mug.

Mrs. Floss watches me pull out my homework and smiles at me. It makes me startle. She's never smiled at me in her entire life. "You look nice today, Sage."

Holy magenta! I think, before recovering and saying, "Um, thank you, Mrs. Floss."

Curtis walks in and drops his green canvas backpack next to his regular seat beside me. Gratitude sprouts in my chest. He could have picked any desk, but he's still willing to sit near me.

"Sorry again about this morning, Curtis." I try to meet his eyes but end up looking at his blue-and-white Nikes. "I was such a jerk."

"We're chill," he says, and he's not even prickly when he says it.

"Really?" I lift my gaze. "Thanks. I swear I mean it. I wasn't myself this morning."

"I know that." His smile is genuine and full of forgiveness. Now I just need to win Bailee over.

My foot is bouncing like crazy. I stop it but start cracking my knuckles. Once Bailee walks in the door and sees that Curtis and I are friends again, she'll sit beside me. I'll show her my lame salamander doodle, and she'll laugh, and all will be well.

Finally, while I'm unloading my pencils, paper, and calculator, she arrives. I sit up. "Look at my lousy doodle." I nervous-laugh.

She doesn't smile. "I'll meet you at the water fountain at lunchtime, Sage." She heads to the far, *far* left corner of the room.

I sink in my chair, my face burning.

Priscilla glides into the room just as the bell rings.

"Priscilla," Mrs. Floss says. "You're tardy." Mrs. Floss uncaps a fat red Sharpie and makes a mark in her book.

Priscilla slips into her front-row seat. "But—"

"Please do not sass me." Mrs. Floss looks over the rim of her glasses. "You need to be seated *before* the bell rings, not while it's ringing."

Whoa. I sit up straight. If Mrs. Floss is going to grump at her favorite student, I don't stand a chance.

Mrs. Floss shuffles papers and catches me watching her. I smile nervously.

And here's the thing. Mrs. Floss smiles back for the second time in her life, teeth and all. The curse is definitely reversing.

"Okay, people," she says. "Trade papers."

Mrs. Floss picks up her mug and begins sipping her soup. I exchange homework sheets with Curtis. We had to write expressions with variables and also evaluate the distributive law of multiplication. I ace everything! And that's pretty much how class goes.

When the end bell rings, I jump from my seat. I don't care if I'm being pushy. Lunchtime is finally here, and I'm ready to clear the air with Bailee.

"Sage," Mrs. Floss says. "Will you stay for a moment, please?"

"Yes, ma'am." I stand by her desk, shifting from foot to foot, watching as Bailee leaves the classroom.

"Nice work with your variables today." Mrs. Floss studies my face. "You really excelled."

"Thank you." My foot taps.

"I was concerned about your work on the geometry unit, but you seem to have a firm grasp on what we're working on now."

I nod, wondering how long this is going to take.

"I do hope you keep it up."

"Yes, ma'am." I glance at the door.

"Okay. Have a nice lunch."

"Thank you." I rush out to meet Bailee at the water fountain. She's not here yet. I line up behind Gigi and Jada. Jada says something about crickets, and the hair on my arms stands on end.

"What's up with that?" I say.

"Hey." Jada turns and smiles at me.

"Is there news on Cricket-gate?" I force a smile, trying to seem casual.

Gigi laughs. "Come on, Sage. It was a good prank." She says this in a friendly tone, not in a mean-girl way. "I'm not going to out you to Mrs. Downy, but everyone knows you were the last one to leave the locker room."

Bailee drops her backpack by our feet, her face telling me she heard everything.

Puce! Sepia! Mauve!

"No," Bailee says. "Didn't you guys leave at the same time?" She looks from Gigi to me.

I swallow. Pressure pulses at the side of my head. "Yeah." My eye twitches.

Gigi laughs. "Okay." She takes a sip from the water fountain.

"Sage?" Bailee says. "You didn't do it. Right?"

"Hey, guys," Hudson says, walking up with Steven and Curtis. "Want to do lunch together again?"

"Sure!" I say, avoiding eye contact with Bailee. I glance at Jada, who's filling her water bottle, at Hudson untwisting his cap, and down the hall. I see Justin walking toward us, and I wave and call, "Hi, Justin."

"Sage?" Bailee says.

I feel sick.

"Mrs. Downy said the crickets came through a hole," I say. "Of course I didn't do this." My eye spasms. I turn to Hudson. "Same table, Hud?"

"Yep. Are you okay?" he asks. "Your eye is freaking out."

"Hey, Sage." Justin joins the group. "What's going on with your eye?"

I want to scream for everybody to shut up about my eye! "It's fine! I got dust in it. Geez." I rub it.

Bailee is quiet, maybe weighing the circumstantial evidence in her head. She's definitely not buying my dust-in-the-eye story.

"Um, Justin, this is everybody. Everyone, this is Justin. He just moved here from Colorado Springs." I wave a shaky hand across the group. Justin says hello and introduces himself person to person. I glance at Bailee again. The air crackles with my guilt. Any minute, my lie is going to unravel.

"So you—" Bailee says as Priscilla walks up.

"What's up?" Priscilla says, interrupting.

"Planning lunch," Hudson says.

"Hey, Priscilla." Jada points down the hall. "Your mom is here and she looks pretty frantic."

"Huh?" Priscilla breaks out of the group and we watch as she heads to her mom. Mrs. Petty says something and Priscilla's chin falls. She cups her hands over her face. Her mom puts an arm around her shoulders, hugs her close, and walks her out the door.

"What do you think that was about?" Justin asks.

Everyone talks at once.

"I don't know," I say.

"I hope she's okay," Bailee says.

"Me too," echo Jada and Gigi.

"It looked kind of serious," I say.

"You guys!" Hudson says, staring at his phone. "I just did a Noodler search. There's something in the local headlines about Goldview First National Bank."

"You think there was another robbery?" Ryan flashes a quick look at me.

I flinch. Mud-colored shame cakes my chest— *shame, shame, shame.*

"My bad, Sage. Sorry," Ryan says. "I didn't mean to bring up a sore subject."

"It's fine."

Justin tries to make eye contact, but I can't.

Bailee squeezes my hand, like aloe on a burn. I exhale and squeeze back.

"Something stormy is up," Steven says.

Hudson clicks more buttons, and Curtis reads the screen over his shoulder.

"Oh no. It's bad." Hudson hands the phone to Steven.

Steven scans it. *"¡Ay, bendito!"*

"What?" we say.

"Priscilla's father"—he clears his throat and puts on his Flores Report voice—"was escorted out of the bank by police and federal agents. He's being investigated for embezzlement!"

CHAPTER 28

After school, Bailee and I jog-walk down Seventh Street, my heart pounding and my words flying a hundred miles a minute. "Minerva has to fix the curse-reverse. It's all a mess—my momma, Priscilla's dad, and us! Our friendship was this close to taking a nosedive!"

"She'll fix it," Bailee says, biting her lower lip.

I'm grateful my best friend is talking to me again and hasn't brought up crickets. Now I offer up a silent prayer that Minerva doesn't mention my quadrupling wish.

We rush across the street, a cool breeze blowing our hair.

We pass Aspen Avenue and Cedar. We walk by the car with the cracked windshield and flat tires. When we near the city bus stop, I see something in Minerva's window. "What is that?"

"I can't tell." Bailee squints.

The "Don't Walk" sign blinks at the crosswalk. A few cars drive past and then we both see it clearly: a big "Closed" sign in Minerva's window!

"Oh no," I scream. "Closed as in closed forever?"

The light changes, and we dash across the street to Minerva's storefront. I grab the door handle and jiggle it even though I know it's locked. Bailee cups her hands around her glasses and peers in the window. "Lights are off."

"Sepia! What if she never comes back?" I drop my backpack to the sidewalk and press my own forehead against the cool glass, trying to see inside.

"The shelves are still stocked," Bailee says. "That's a good sign."

"Yeah, but why the closed sign in the middle of the day? Why not a sign that says, 'I'll be back at five' or whenever?" My voice rises. "This is the kind of thing that happens in books, you know?"

Bailee steps away from the window. "What?"

I begin pacing back and forth, my feet crunching down on scattered leaves. "Magic portals. They always disappear at the worst possible time. Right? Didn't that sort of thing happen in *The Golden Compass* and in *The Unicorn Chronicles*? And, spoiler alert, it happens in the Chronicles of Narnia series."

"Stop!" Bailee holds her hands over her ears. "I haven't read the Narnia series yet!"

"I'm just saying, what if that's what's happening in real life?"

"Don't stress. This isn't the time to freak out. You're going to be fine."

"Liar. I've seen that look on your face all day, Bailee. Don't pretend you're feeling Zen!"

"The look you've been seeing all day," Bailee pops her hands to her hips, "is me not liking the new you."

"Sorry. Geez." I huff. "I'm tired of apologizing for everything." I exhale a long breath and continue pacing back and forth.

"Listen." Bailee lets her arms fall to her sides. "I've been thinking about a loophole. How about if you make another wish to reverse the curse so it circles right back to the beginning, returning to the way things were? That way you're not technically unwishing the wish."

I think for a moment and say, "I like that you're thinking of a loophole, but that wish might be the same as unwishing, and if it is, it'll have the same consequences as unwishing." I stomp on a pinecone. "I'd really just love to wish the whole curse away." My voice spins high and fast. "It actually scares me to wish for anything without Minerva's help now that we're seeing how lousy the curse-reverse is turning out."

Bailee nods.

"Seriously. Who knows what I'll lose if I make another curse wish—I mean, Minerva probably knows, but she's not here." My panic escalates. I rush back to the window and peer inside again. The store is still dark. "She may never come back!"

"We'll figure it out." Gray shades of worry color Bailee's words.

I sink down to sit on the curb and pick up a leaf from the gutter. "You think I'll ever be artistic again?"

"Of course I do." Bailee sits beside me.

A noisy city bus with an "Out of Service" sign rumbles past.

"I have to be careful with my last two wishes," I say. "After sunset on Friday, I won't have any more chances to fix things." I let out a pitiful *ugh* sound. "What's more, if we do ever see Minerva again, I'm worried about how she'll fix the curse-reverse, because if I'm being honest—I don't want Mr. Petty in jail, but I don't want my daddy in jail, either."

"What about wishing him out of jail?"

I sigh. "Yeah, I've been thinking about that, but I need to ask Minerva exactly how to word that wish." My quadrupling wish was a disaster. "Words matter. I don't want to say the wish wrong and have my daddy out of jail but marked down as an escapee. Or what if I make the wish and the prison doors fly open, and a bunch of real criminals run off, too?"

My brain hurts trying to figure it all out. I ball up the leaf I'm holding until broken pieces crumble to the ground. I bang my fist into my palm. "I just wish my daddy weren't connected to Momma's curse so he could go free."

"What if . . ." Bailee clears her throat and gently says, "Um. What if your dad being in jail has nothing to do with the curse?"

Hot tears sting the backs of my eyes.

"Or, I don't know." Bailee hurries and adds, "Maybe it does." She gently bumps my knee against hers. "Do you want to come over to my house, and we can try to figure out what to do next, and then maybe come back here in a few hours to see if Minerva returns?"

"It'll be dark."

"My mom could drive us," Bailee offers.

I sniffle. "I don't know. I sort of want to go home."

A loud horn honks down at the end of the street, another city bus. A car squeals out in front of it. The

229

bus stops at a red light. "Hey," Bailee says. "Let's take the bus. Forget my house and your apartment. Let's go somewhere neutral. Maybe it'll help us think with clear heads."

"Okay. How about the Goldview Café?"

"Perfect!" Bailee agrees. We scoop up our backpacks and run across the street as the bus pulls up. "We'll figure out the loopholes in the magic once and for all."

CHAPTER 29

We climb on the bus, show the driver our student IDs since students ride free, and take the front-row seat. For the record, the city bus seats are cushier than the ones on our school bus and the windows are bigger, but it smells like diesel and there's no good music.

"If Miss Tammy is working, we can sit in one of her booths," I say. "I have eight dollars in my back pocket from my birthday money. We can get a couple of Snowy Sodas and maybe some fries."

"Thanks! What did you spend the other two dollars on?"

Crickets, I think. "Oh, um, I don't remember. Gum

or something like that."

"I'd love a piece." Bailee is looking out the window back at Minerva's.

"Huh?"

"Of gum."

"Oh . . . I'm out."

"You chewed the whole pack already?" Bailee turns to me.

"Yeah." I crack my knuckles.

"I would have loved to have seen that bubble, you gum hog."

I force a laugh.

Five minutes later, we're outside the café. The trees have shed about three-quarters of their hold, and amber-gold leaves line the path to the entrance.

Bailee swings open the glass café door. It smells like coffee and buttery waffles even though it's four o'clock in the afternoon. "Well, looky-looky," Miss Tammy says with a big smile. "It's Lil' Spice and Bay Leaf."

"Hi, Miss Tammy," we say.

She drops her pad into her black apron pocket and puts an arm over my shoulders. "Come have a seat in one of my booths."

"Hey!" Bailee waves at someone. "There's Priscilla."

"Seriously?" I don't bother to hide the grouch in my tone. Godzilla is sitting just three spots over from the shiny red booth Miss Tammy leads us to. "Payne's gray," I grumble.

Bailee rolls her eyes.

"You'll be fine," Miss Tammy says. She knows all about Priscilla and me.

If Godzilla gives me any grief, I'm ready with a comeback about how her daddy can take my daddy's cell when they set him free, and welcome to Club Infamous. Let's see how she likes it now.

Then I notice her red-rimmed eyes and puffy cheeks, and I can't help but feel a little sorry for her. Priscilla gives Bailee a halfhearted wave before staring down at her paper placemat.

Bailee and I scoot into our booth, and Miss Tammy hands each of us a plastic menu.

"Where's her mom?" Bailee asks quietly.

Miss Tammy lowers her voice. "Well, Priscilla is not seated in my section. That's one of Jenny's tables, but I do know she came here with a friend." Miss Tammy scoots in on my side of the booth and whispers even lower. "Jenny says the friend's mother showed up and said the girl needed to leave ASAP. By the look on that mother's face, I'd say she didn't want her daughter being seen in public with Priscilla—at least not today. You heard the news, right?"

We both nod. My chest feels hollow.

233

Miss Tammy goes on. "I think Priscilla noticed that mother's unfriendly face, too, poor thing, but she acted nonchalant, and when the friend offered her a ride, Priscilla said she wanted to stay a little longer and offered to pay the bill."

"Uh-huh," I say.

"So," Miss Tammy says, "the friend leaves and Priscilla tries paying with her mother's credit card, but it's declined and so Priscilla tells Jenny that her mom is on the way to pay. She's been sitting there ever since." Miss Tammy pauses. "Come to think about it, I'll bet the bank froze all the Pettys' accounts."

I glance at Priscilla's face and think of how sick I felt when I heard about my own daddy.

"Order up," someone calls from the kitchen.

Miss Tammy stands. "Lou needs me to deliver food. I'll be right back."

I lean forward to Bailee and whisper, "If the curse-reverse is in full force, her mother is not going to show up. The battery in their fancy car is going to die, and she's never going to find any money. Priscilla's going to be sitting there until closing. Unless . . ."

I stand up.

"What are you doing?" Bailee asks, standing too.

"I don't know," I say. "Just give me a minute to talk to her by myself."

I walk over to Priscilla's table.

"Hello, Weed," she says without energy.

"Hi, Zilla," I say in a soft voice.

She picks up her mostly empty water glass and a few ice cubes clink around. The bill on the table has *$6.45* written in blue ink. Priscilla sips the final drops of water and sets down her glass. Ten awkward seconds pass without a word and then I say, "Um—"

Miss Tammy delivers an armful of food to a nearby table and gives me a worried glance.

"Go ahead." Priscilla crosses her arms. "Give me your best shot. I would if I were you."

"Um, I'm wondering if you'd like to sit with me and Bailee."

"What?" She searches my face. "Why?"

"Because I know how you feel." I take the eight dollars from my pocket and slide it under the bill. "Come on. Truce. At least for today."

I turn on my heels and walk to my booth without giving Priscilla a chance to argue or say anything. She follows me and quietly scoots in on Bailee's side.

"Hey?" Bailee says, looking back and forth between us.

"Hi." Priscilla's voice is barely audible.

I wink at Bailee, letting her know everything is okay.

Priscilla watches Jenny clear her table and pick up the wad of bills. "Thanks," Priscilla says quietly.

I shrug. "No problem."

"I didn't know what I'd do—" Priscilla's voice catches and it's about to turn awkward, but Miss Tammy walks up.

"May we have waters, Miss Tammy?" I ask.

Miss Tammy's eyes are shiny. She clears her throat and says, "Sure thing. By the way, Lou accidently made an extra batch of French fries. Would you girls take them off our hands?"

"That'd be great!"

Bailee is grinning from ear to ear, perhaps about the free food, but I suspect it's about me and Priscilla finally getting along.

Miss Tammy sets a hot batch of salty fries in front of us. Bailee and I dip ours in ketchup, and Priscilla dips hers in mayonnaise. We eat one after another until they're gone. Maybe I'm drunk on French fries, or maybe it's desperation and good cheer that inspires me with a new idea. I lean across the booth and say, "Listen, you're probably not going to believe me, but for my birthday I wished . . ." I pause and look at Bailee.

She gives me a nod to go on.

"I wished on a magic candle that the curse between our families would reverse."

Priscilla stays surprisingly quiet as I tell her about Minerva's candle, and my theory about basketball, art, and Momma.

"I also think the curse-reverse is responsible for what's happening now and why your daddy was taken to jail. I didn't mean for that to happen," I say. "Maybe if we team up, we can fix this together and free both of our daddies."

Priscilla's face stays blank.

"I know the idea of a magic candle sounds incredible," Bailee says to Priscilla. "But trust me. I've seen it in action with my own eyes."

Priscilla shifts and blinks a few times. "Well," she says thoughtfully before fast-talking, "my mother has been really sweet lately, and my father is not in jail anymore. Mother bailed him out this afternoon, so everything with my father is going to be fine. He promised me that the accountants at the bank would figure out their mistake by morning."

They won't, I think. *And bail is only temporary.*

"I know you're having a hard time believing all this," I say, realizing she hasn't made one comment about the candle or magic. That's fair. It sounds pretty farfetched.

I'm about to explain further when Priscilla says, "About the truce. Are you serious?"

"One hundred percent," I say. "All is forgiven. The jabs, the pickles, the mustache drawn on my photo, everything. So truce?"

"Deal," she says sincerely. "And I forgive you for the crickets."

I freeze.

"It's okay," Priscilla says. "Mrs. Snyder already gossiped to my mom about how you bought the crickets at the pet store. I mean, it sucked having that prank played on me, but it was clever and I would have done it to you if I'd thought of it first."

Bailee goes stiff.

My mouth is frozen. I've never seen Bailee look so . . . so . . . so everything—upset, disappointed, heartbroken, hurt, angry—all at once.

Other than the contorting of her face, Bailee doesn't move a muscle. A small noise leaves her throat and then there's no sound. She's silent for what feels like forever until, "I'm such a dummy!" She pauses for a moment before adding, "No wonder you already knew Justin! And you were the last one to leave the gym. I'm supposed to be your best friend, and you've been lying to me for three days straight." She's screaming now. "You even just lied to me in the last hour." She turns to Priscilla. "I need out of this booth."

Priscilla sits there, stunned.

"Move," Bailee screams. "I said I want out."

People in the café dart looks our way.

Priscilla scoots, and Bailee climbs past her. I think Bailee is going to march out of the café but she puts her hands on her hips and says, "You didn't spend two dollars on gum, did you?"

I rise to my feet, trying to think of a way to make this right.

"I trusted you. I was blind about you causing Cricket-gate because I trusted you!"

"Bailee, please let me explain." I reach for her arm to give her our BFF squeeze, but she jerks away from me.

"I'm sorry." Priscilla looks between us. "I honestly thought Bailee knew."

"Right," I snap before I turn back to Bailee. "Bay . . ." I take a step forward, trying to reach out to her again.

"Stay away from me." Her words sting. "You know I hate bugs. You know germs are my worst nightmare." Her eyes grow bigger. "Or do you? Maybe you're too focused on yourself and your stupid curse that you never even bothered to consider how a bug prank would be the most selfish and mean thing anyone has ever done to me." She throws her arms up and makes a crazy laugh. "I can't believe this."

"I'm sorry. I'm really, really sorry."

Bailee storms out, but not before saying, "Our friendship is over, Sage. *O-V-E-R,* over!"

I turn to Priscilla, ready to explode red-hot lava.

"I am so, *so* sorry, Sage." She folds her arms over her stomach. "I didn't know she didn't know. I thought that's why you guys were fighting the other day. I thought you'd told Bailee everything." Her eyes tell me she's telling the truth.

The rage dies in my mouth. This is my own fault. I should never have done the cricket prank, and I should never have wished for a curse-reverse.

"Sepia," I say, my voice low. I drop my chin to my chest.

Priscilla's phone beeps. "I have to go. My mom is here."

I picture Mrs. Petty sitting outside the café in her shiny black car, maybe on the phone with her fancy lawyer, discussing how they're sure they'll win Mr. Petty's case, how her daddy will come home and mine will stay in jail. The Petty family will come out on top once again.

Now more than ever would be a good time to stop waiting for the curse-reverse and wish Daddy out of jail before he's stuck behind bars for good. That, plus winning Doodle for Noodler, is what I really need.

"Thanks again for paying my check," Priscilla says as she hurries toward the door. "I owe you one." Dried dirt-brown leaves flutter and a gush of cold rushes through the café door.

The solstice is coming, and I am blizzard-white alone.

CHAPTER 30

Miss Tammy calls Momma to let her know I'll finish my homework at the restaurant and we'll ride the bus home together. Then she serves me a bowl of what my daddy calls the café's "famous" chili. I think he's the only one who calls it famous, but it is really good. The chili is meaty and has beans, big chunks of tomato, and just the right amount of salt and peppery spices. Miss Tammy also brings me a square of warm cornbread with creamy butter melting on top.

More than I deserve.

It's dark outside when we finally climb on the cold bus. "Why so quiet, darling?" Miss Tammy says.

"Those chili beans getting to you, or are you still sulking about your fight with Bailee?"

"Bailee," I say, staring out the tall window. Silver stars glitter high above the mountaintops. I wonder if Bailee is looking out her bedroom window at the same stars. I wonder if my daddy is, too, or if his prison cell even has a window.

"I'm sorry." She pauses. "You want to talk about it?"

"No, ma'am." I keep staring out the window.

"That was really sweet what you did for Priscilla."

"Thanks." Just then, a shooting star dashes across the blue-black sky. I catch my breath and hold it, making a wish right away.

I wish my life would go back to normal, I say in my head.

Just to make sure I'm not imagining things, I say, "Did you see that, Miss Tammy?"

"I saw it, sugar."

The bus rumbles and glides past Minerva's, the store still dark. But I saw a shooting star! That has to count for something. I turn to Miss Tammy. "Do you believe wishes on shooting stars come true?"

"Well, sure I do." She pauses before adding, "I also believe people can make their own magic. A lot of times, folks wait around for something supernatural to happen when a little effort could do the same trick."

She smiles at me. "I bet you have magic in you."

I smile back. I also have a shooting-star wish. My tension lightens. If I can have magic from a candle, why not a shooting star? Maybe I'll walk into my apartment, and Momma will be back to normal.

The bus bumps along.

And maybe I'll sketch a Noodler logo tonight, and it will be great. Maybe it'll be extra good—even the best drawing of my life! *And*, I think, sitting up tall, *since shooting-star magic is probably more powerful than candle magic, maybe Bailee will be waiting in my apartment, ready to forgive me, and I'll promise to never do anything horrible again, and she'll know she can trust me. And maybe Daddy's lawyer will have figured out something new with his case and we'll get a phone call saying he's coming home tomorrow!*

I wriggle in my seat, wanting to urge the bus driver to step on it. Things are going to be good again. And I still have two wishes and two days with my candle. Even though I don't know what I need to wish for by the solstice, I could use one wish to figure it out.

When we arrive at our stop, I hurry Miss Tammy off the bus and up the apartment stairs. "Bye," I say, twirling and rushing past her apartment to mine.

She laughs. "Glad to see your mood has lifted."

I turn the knob and swing open the door, confident

Bailee will be on the other side. Instead, there's a bunch of large brown moving boxes scattered in the living room and kitchen.

"Hello?" I call, shutting the door.

"Back here," Momma says. "In my room."

I push aside the boxes blocking the entrance and walk inside her bedroom. Momma stands by her closet, folds a flower-print blouse, and places it in a box.

"What's going on?" I ask.

"What does it look like?" Momma says with a Mrs. Petty tone. "We're moving out of this gossipy town."

"But—"

"And there's more good news." Momma takes a pair of black pants from a hanger, her tone changing to somewhere between sweet and businesslike. "I hired a better lawyer, and she is certain the court will hear your daddy's appeal. She has discovered that flagrant prosecutorial misconduct took place during the original trial."

I don't understand all of Momma's words, but I heard "better lawyer" and "daddy," so I nod and listen.

"She feels certain that your daddy will go free and will probably not have to face a retrial after the ill-gotten evidence is thrown out."

It's more proof of the curse-reverse—Priscilla's

daddy arrested and mine on the verge of coming home. You'd think I'd be jumping up and down, but my stomach knots up with words that itch to leave my tongue.

"What is it?" Momma asks.

"And the new lawyer will prove he's innocent, right?"

"Oh, honey." She stops folding the black pants and sets them on her dresser. Her overcautious tone and sad eyes make my chest tighten.

"What?"

"Well," she says softly, "I think it's important that you and I are truthful with each other. Don't you?"

"Why are you asking me that?" My defensive tone buzzes between us.

"Sweetheart." She tucks a loose strand of hair behind her ear. "Have you opened any of the letters Daddy sent to you?"

"No, I . . ." A squeak chokes my throat. I suddenly want to tell her to do what she always does—pretend, ignore, dance around the subject. "Never mind."

"Sage, honey. He did it. Your daddy tried to rob that bank. He broke in at night and was caught."

Her words knock the breath out of me. "What?" I sink onto the edge of her soft beige bedspread.

She sits beside me and we stay quiet for a few moments.

"Why would he do that?" I whisper.

Momma sighs. "He'd just been laid off and was worried about money. He told me he did it because he didn't want us to lose the house." She shakes her head. "I wish he would have trusted me enough to talk to me."

My head spins. Momma is not making sense. Daddy is the talker, not Momma. And Daddy wouldn't have done this.

"But like I said, our new lawyer discovered a few things, so cross your fingers he gets released."

"You're wrong, Momma." I stand up. "You're lying!" I run to my room and yank open my dresser drawer. I pull out Daddy's letters and rip one open. It'll be an explanation. His proclamation of innocence.

The first line after "Dear Sage" says, "I'm sorry I did this to our family." I rip into the next letter. Five lines down, it reads, "I take full ownership." Deep in the next letter, he writes, "Please forgive me. I'll spend my life making this up to you."

The truth was there all along, tucked away in my drawer, but it still shocks and stings like a belly flop. I crumble to my bed and shred the letters into confetti, tears streaming down my face. My heart sinks below my comforter, below the box springs, and below the dusty tan carpet. Just when it feels like I could get swallowed by an ocean of grief, Momma comes and sits down beside me, leg to leg. She takes hold of my hands. "Sage, we'll survive this together." She leans her head on mine and hugs me tight. "Your daddy is a good man. He made a dumb decision."

We stay leg to leg, hand in hand, for a long while.

When my crying comes to an end, Momma wipes my tears with her thumb. "A move will be good. We'll leave Goldview, where everybody is in everyone's business." An edge seeps into her tone, her own hurt. She stands up and adds, "I, for one, am ready to say good riddance to people like Mrs. Snyder and others who spend their time gossiping about us and the curse." From my doorway she adds, "Why don't you put on some deodorant and come help me pack?"

I shudder at how quickly the sharpness creeps back into Momma's tone. The Mrs. Petty voice. The curse-reverse is still alive. It might be giving me my daddy back, but it's taking Momma in the process, and now she wants us to move!

I can't take it anymore. I need to fix my mess-up— with or without Minerva's help, I need to use one of my last two wishes to try Bailee's idea on the loophole and wish for another curse-reverse so it circles back to how things were. Even if we lose the money, the lawyers have already found the problems in Daddy's case, so he'll still get released. My candle can still fix everything. It has to.

I hurry to the kitchen and whip open the drawer.

Empty?

It's empty!

I grab the brown box labeled "Kitchen" and peel back the tape. Dishes, cups, silverware. But nothing from the junk drawer.

"Momma," I holler, and run back to her bedroom. "Momma, where is the stuff from the kitchen drawer?"

"What are you talking about?" She takes a blue Sharpie and writes "Bedroom" across a box full of clothes.

"Momma, please think," I say, desperate. "Where is the stuff from the kitchen drawers. I'm looking for my candle from my birthday."

"The junk drawer?" Momma says. "I threw all that stuff out this morning. The flashlight didn't work. The pencils were broken. The candles were used."

I rush to the kitchen and rummage through the garbage can.

Momma follows me. "We aren't poor anymore, Sage. I upended the drawer into the trash can and brought it down to the dumpster."

"Momma!"

She takes the garbage can from my hand. "What has gotten into you? We'll buy new stuff."

I run out the apartment door and hustle down the

stairs. The parking lot lights shine on the reflective sign posted to the side of the Dumpster:

NO UNAUTHORIZED DUMPING. FOR USE BY BEAR CREEK APARTMENT RESIDENTS ONLY. WEEKLY PICKUP, WEDNESDAYS, 5:00 P.M.

Wednesdays! Five p.m.! As in, the time I was at the diner!

But maybe the garbage pickup ran late today.

I push up the lid. The Dumpster releases the foul smell of dirt, grease, and rot. But aside from a brown-black banana peel, it's empty.

CHAPTER 31 ✴
✴ THURSDAY, DECEMBER 20

On Thursday morning's bus ride, Bailee won't look at me. She and Curtis sit even closer to the front than Gigi, all golden and happy. I sit in my seat, blizzard-white alone. The pine-scented air feels even cooler than yesterday. I zip up my navy-blue hoodie. Brown leaves droop and then flutter down to the gutter, and I think the end of a season might also be the end of my friendship. Nothing gold can stay.

When we arrive at school, Bailee doesn't go to our lockers with me; instead she hurries to PE on her own.

A "One day until the solstice!" sign hangs sideways from my locker door. I'm ripping it down when Priscilla grabs my elbow and whispers, "Sage." Panic flows from her voice. "I need to talk to you."

"Okay?" I say.

We step to a less busy spot in the hallway, near the teachers' lounge. I lean against the dove-white wall and students rush by, hurrying to class.

"The police took my father back to jail this morning on additional charges." Priscilla's eyes glisten. "It's just like you said about the curse-reverse going wonky on our families. I think the wishes messed us up."

"So, you believe in my magic candle?"

"*Our* magic candles."

"Huh?" I say.

She looks side to side and whispers, "I got a twelfth candle, too."

"From Minerva's!" I holler. Passing students turn their heads toward us.

"*Shhhh.*" Priscilla pulls me into the small teachers' lounge that smells like roasted coffee beans. There's a table, four chairs, and a counter with a coffeepot making brewing and dripping sounds, but we're alone, standing inches apart.

"You got a candle from Minerva's?" I repeat.

"Yes." Priscilla shuts the door and leans against it.

"Do you still have it?" My eardrums pulse.

"No," she says quickly. "My mother doesn't save anything. She threw it away with the rest of my birthday candles, so I only had the chance to make one wish."

"Why would you let her throw it away!"

The coffeepot hisses and steams.

"I thought Minerva was a nutjob. I had no idea the candle was really magical until you told me everything that happened to you."

Beep. Beep. Beep. The coffee maker's blue "ready" light blinks.

"We should talk somewhere else." I reach for the door handle. "Somebody is going to come for their morning java."

"We're fine." Priscilla locks the door.

"All right." I drop my arm to my side, heart racing. "What did you wish for?"

"Almost same as you," she says. "I wanted what you called it, a curse-reverse."

"Why would you want that?" Shock makes my voice rise. "You have everything."

"*Shhh.*"

The door handle jiggles. *Knock, knock.* "Hello?" We hear Mrs. Rimmels's voice on the other side of the door. "Anyone in there? I think you accidently locked the door."

Priscilla whispers, "Your mom is so nice." A single tear trails down her cheek. "Your mom hugs you and laughs with you and doesn't care that your hair looks like that all the time."

"Hey!" I run a hand over my hair and smooth down a lump in my ponytail.

"My mom." Priscilla drops her chin and lets out a big exhale. "She probably means well and has some good days, but most times she nags at me about anything and everything. It feels like no matter what I do, I'll never be good enough. I try hard, trust me— making the basketball team, competing in math, keeping my room clean. I don't even have time to read or do the things I want to do because I can't keep up, and it doesn't matter anyhow. I'm never good enough." Priscilla sniffles. "Your mom is sweet and you get to ride the bus home with everyone, and you always win the chocolate donut. It's not fair that the curse gave you the better deal."

"Whoa!" I take a moment to try and wrap my brain around what she's saying. "You get loads of gifts, and ride around in a fancy car, and I'll bet your refrigerator is always stocked."

"Yeah, so?" Priscilla looks confused.

"Trust me," I say, "when your refrigerator is empty, these things matter."

The bell rings.

"Okay," I say. "Regardless, you're telling me you

wished for a curse-reverse, too?"

"Not exactly. I wished for pink lightning to strike again. I thought that would get rid of the curse for good."

"Oooooo, better! But wasn't your party on Saturday?" I say, thinking about the rules of the candle and how Minerva said no wishing on Saturdays or Sundays.

"Yeah?" Priscilla scrunches her eyebrows together.

The door jiggles again. "Hello?" This time it's Mrs. Downy's voice. Keys jingle on the other side of the door.

The doorknob twists.

In walk Mrs. Downy and Mrs. Rimmels.

"They're all yours," Mrs. Downy says to Mrs. Rimmels. She drops the keys into the pocket of her tan pants. "I need to inspect bags at the gym. I'll be waiting for you two."

"Girls?" Mrs. Rimmels crinkles her eyebrows together.

We gulp.

"Care to explain?"

The door clicks shut and Mrs. Rimmels turns up her hearing aids.

"It's about the Contrarium Curse," I say.

The wrinkles on her face soften.

"We want it to end," Priscilla says.

I add, "Will you please help us?"

Mrs. Rimmels grabs each of us by a hand and squeezes. "I thought you'd never ask."

CHAPTER 32

We're already late for gym, but we don't care. Priscilla and I stay in the teachers' lounge with Mrs. Rimmels.

She squeezes our hands again and says, "The curse has gone on long enough. I'm so delighted you two want to put it to rest." She lets go of our hands and pours coffee into a bone-white cup; steam rises from the center. "As you are aware, I have known your mothers since they were young girls, and I have seen this curse since its very beginning. It has been sad to witness their actions, two sweet friends turning against each other." She adds cream to her coffee. "Forgive me for saying so, but instead of your mothers showing their usual generosity, they turned quite selfish in the Contrarium race." Mrs. Rimmels *tsks* and scoops sugar into her coffee. She stirs, the spoon clinking on the edge of the cup. She places her cup on the table, slides out a chair, and sits. "Join me."

Priscilla and I sit side by side across from her.

Mrs. Rimmels sips her coffee, her lipstick leaving pink on the rim. "I have spent years and years researching the curse, until the key to ending it finally occurred to me." She takes another sip, her hands a bit shaky. "Contrarium is the Curse of Opposites, so what is the opposite of selfish?"

Priscilla and I stay quiet and wait for the answer.

"Well, come on, girls, this is not a rhetorical question. Give me an antonym for 'selfish.'"

"Um, generous or kind," I say.

"Yes. Exactly, Sage! Generous. And I love that you've added kind in there, too." She sets her cup on the table. "That's good for extra points—however, not enough to reach Priscilla's tally." She smiles at Priscilla. "You'll see in class you've won this week's Friday donut. I brought it today since school is closed tomorrow for the solstice celebration."

"Nice job, Priscilla," I manage to say.

Surprise glows across Priscilla's face.

"Since generosity and kindness are opposites of selfishness and mean-spiritedness, I believe you'll need to show a generous act of kindness in order for the curse to break."

"Not to brag, Mrs. Rimmels," I loop an arm over Priscilla's shoulders, "but I was kind to Priscilla yesterday."

"She was!" Priscilla nods fast. "She paid my bill at the café!"

"I'm so happy to hear this, girls. Did anything change with the curse?"

I think of Priscilla's dad's arrest and my momma's snippy tone. "No." I set my hands back in my lap. "Unless by 'change' you mean has it gotten worse. Then the answer is yes."

Mrs. Rimmels's face pinches like something's not right, and then she says, "Perhaps if your mothers had chosen a kind act like that years ago, the curse would've been easier to break." She picks up her cup again. "But I suspect since this curse has been going on for more than a few decades, you'll need several kind acts to solidify the job."

"Anything else?" I ask.

"Hmm." Mrs. Rimmels sips again. "I'm sure you two are smart enough to figure it out."

Priscilla and I exchange looks. It's almost like Mrs. Rimmels knows more than she's saying.

"So we don't need any magic or special weather?" I ask. "You're saying just be kind?"

"You'll only know if you try." She sips. "I do hope you'll get busy. You only have until the solstice to figure it out."

"Until the solstice?" Priscilla says. "As in, tomorrow's solstice?"

"That's right," she says. "Otherwise, you'll have to wait until you have children and then wait until it's your son's or daughter's twelfth birthday, and hope they can eliminate the curse. This is your in-between year, so it's your one chance."

Priscilla looks as confused as I feel. "Are you serious? We have to break the curse by tomorrow or we're stuck with it for decades?"

"I'd never joke about something like this," Mrs. Rimmels says. "It's just the way of curses. Families are given one chance per generation to fix the disasters of the previous generation. I hope you don't blow your opportunity."

"You think we can break it without pink lightning?" I ask.

"I can't say for sure. Life doesn't come with guarantees." Mrs. Rimmels taps her gold watch. "Oh, goodness me. We must have missed the bell."

"But—" I say.

"You're very, *very* late, girls. Hurry to class before you get detention."

"Can't you write a late pass for us?" I ask.

"Well, of course I can, but I won't, since you chose to help yourselves to the teachers' lounge and lock the door rather than coming to me in the first place."

Mrs. Rimmels points a crooked finger to the door. "Run along, now."

Priscilla and I scoop up our bags and rush to the gym.

"What do you think?" Priscilla asks, fast-walking beside me.

"I think Mrs. Rimmels is the smartest person in town."

"Me too."

We run around the corner. Mrs. Downy is still waiting outside the gym door. She checks our bags and then we speed into the locker room, change, and hurry out to the basketball court. Bouncing balls pound the floor. Bailee turns away when she sees me.

"Welcome, ladies," Coach says, and even though it's noisy, her sarcasm is loud and clear. "Glad you could join us." She looks at her sports watch. "You two are unreasonably late. That will cost you fifteen burpees each, and after-school detention."

"Coach," Priscilla says, "it was my fault. Not Sage's."

I gulp, thinking how a detention will disqualify me from the Noodler competition. I'll lose my chance of going from infamous to famous. "Please, Coach. How about thirty burpees instead of detention?" I say. "And don't punish Priscilla. I'm the one who took so long talking to Mrs. Rimmels."

"No," Priscilla says, "I'm the one who caused the delay."

Basketballs have stopped bouncing and the gym is silent. Everyone is looking at us. Jada and Gigi prop balls against their hips and stare. Even Bailee can't help but watch.

"Honestly, Coach, I'm the one who's always late," I say. "Maybe instead of detention I could run laps—"

Coach blows her whistle. "Fine. Laps! Both of you. Until the end of PE."

"But—"

"Go, or I'll make everyone run." Gigi and Jada shoot us looks that beg us to *Move it!*

Priscilla and I start running around the perimeter of the basketball court, and Coach blows her whistle at the rest of the class. "Everyone else, back to drills."

Bailee turns her back to me and dribbles.

"We can do it," I say to Priscilla. "We can do kindness."

"Yeah," Priscilla says in between breaths. "But how will we know when it's enough?"

Tweeeeeet. Coach's whistle dangles at her chest.

"Petty. Sassafras. No talking! You don't get rewarded with social hour when you're late."

We clamp our mouths shut and run in silence, me wondering if little acts of kindness will be enough after so many years of meanness. How do we make up for a generation of evil looks, exclusion, and pranks?

Thirty-two minutes later, sweat dots my chest and forehead. My underarms feel damp. Our running has slackened to a slow jog-walk and I'm breathing hard. We continue making laps around the perimeter with our lips sealed. I keep wondering how we'll fix the curse.

When the whistle blows to end PE, Priscilla and I are on the far end of the gym. I let out a huge breath and sink to the floor. "Finally."

Priscilla folds forward and dangles her arms to the ground. "It feels like we ran twelve miles."

"Yeah." I laugh. "At least."

I watch as Bailee and the rest of the girls pick up loose balls and put them away; still no eye contact from my BFF.

After taking a few more breaths, Priscilla stands and offers me a hand up. I look at her outstretched palm. Two days ago, there's no way I would have taken it, but now I grab it, and she helps me to my feet.

"I feel so gross." I tug my damp shirt away from my neck.

"Yeah." She fans herself.

"Hey," I say as we walk across the gym floor, "I was thinking maybe our kind acts alone won't be enough."

Priscilla cocks an eyebrow. "Okay?"

"Think about it," I say. "A lot of people in Goldview have either taken a side in the curse, gossiped about it, or at least have an opinion about it, so maybe we need to involve the community to help fix it."

Priscilla picks up a rolling basketball and sets it on the shelf with other balls. "How would involving others help us?"

I stoop and pick up a stray ball. "I'm not exactly sure." I remember what Miss Tammy said about making my own magic and say, "Here's the thing. A lightning bolt is energy, right? It's what sparked the curse, but we've kept it alive. And so has the town. Maybe a bunch of community kindness will give us enough energy to help lift it."

"Um?" Priscilla says, and in that single word I can tell she's not convinced. She picks up another ball and sets it on the shelf.

I gently grab her arm and say, "It's like Mrs. Rimmels said: there are no guarantees. We've got to try."

Priscilla shrugs. "Okay." With more enthusiasm she adds, "And we have my wish for pink lightning as backup."

"Yeah." I try to sound positive, but I can't help but think Priscilla didn't have Bailee by her side listening to the list of rules. "Did you use your candle on Friday for your real birthday, or Saturday at your party?"

"Saturday," Priscilla says. "Why?"

"Just curious." I try to sound casual instead of deflated. But who knows if Priscilla got the same instructions as me. Maybe she was allowed weekend wishes. I force a smile to my face and say, "It's going to work out for us."

I set the ball on the shelf, scanning the gym for Bailee, and see the back of her head as she goes into the locker room. Jada and Gigi walk over. "What's up with you two?" Jada asks.

Priscilla throws a sweaty arm over my shoulder. "We called a truce."

"Yep," I confirm.

Gigi's eyebrows pop up.

"Thank goodness!" Jada flings her arms in the air and does a cheerleader jump. "Finally! All your bickering has been making me so uptight."

"I knew it!" Gigi says. "I mean, I'm surprised, but I still knew it! Didn't I predict this, Jada?"

"Yep!" Jada says.

"I saw you guys duck into the teachers' lounge, and I just had a good feeling!" Gigi says.

"Okay." I chuckle, except she's right. She was usually right about stuff when we hung out.

The four of us are smiling as we walk into the locker room. Bailee is already changing, so I sit near her, hoping for another chance to talk. But Bailee scoops up her clothing and moves around the corner, disappearing behind a new aisle of lockers.

My heart fills with inky blackness.

"You okay?" Priscilla says to me.

I shake my head.

"Is there anything I can do?" she asks.

"I need a minute."

Priscilla, Jada, and Gigi take their washcloths to the sinks.

I grab my towel and head to the shower room. I almost never shower after PE, but running laps and my momma's talk about deodorant have me self-conscious. I push aside the plastic curtain, turn on the water, and wait for it to warm. Only one other girl showers, Shanie, and we each pick a stall far apart. I use rose-scented soap from the dispenser, and five minutes later I'm done and drying off. Shanie is already gone.

When I return to the changing room, it's empty except for Gigi.

"Hey." Gigi hugs her royal-blue sweater to her

chest. "I didn't know you were still here."

I turn my back to give her privacy and open my locker. "I needed to smell a little better."

"Yeah." She laughs. "For Justin?"

"No." I laugh, too, because I think she's right.

"He's cute and a seventh grader!"

"We're going to the dance together." I'm not sure if that's exactly true, but I like saying it. I pull on my underwear and new jeans.

"That's great," Gigi says.

It feels good to be talking like we used to back when we were friends.

"Um," she says. "I know it's been a while, but do you want to come over on Friday? To get ready."

I slip on my bra and shirt. "Really?" I turn toward Gigi.

"Yeah."

"I guess that means you heard about my daddy's appeal."

"What?" Gigi brushes her long dark hair.

"My daddy's appeal with the courts. How they're probably letting him out of . . . you know."

"That's cool. No. I hadn't heard." She brushes through her hair one more time and then sweeps up the left side, clipping it in place with a barrette.

"You haven't?"

"No. Why?" Gigi clangs her locker door shut and places her brush on the bench.

"Because you just asked me to come over on Friday." I pause.

"Yeah?" Gigi looks at me, confused.

"Isn't my daddy the reason you stopped hanging out with me?"

"Oh." Gigi looks down and fiddles with her thumb cuticle. "That's what you think?"

"Okay?" I shove my wet towel and dirty clothing into a plastic bag and tie it shut at the top. "Why did you stop hanging out with me and Bailee?"

"The truth?" Gigi sits on the bench.

"Duh. I'm not asking for a lie!"

"Hmm." Gigi crosses her arms. "Really? Because you haven't minded lies lately. At least when you're asking me to cover for you about who left the locker room when." Gigi looks ready to say more but stops herself, takes a breath, and sighs it out. Her face softens. "I'm sorry. That sounded snotty, and I really want to say this right. I've held on to this for a long time, and I want you to hear the truth, because I think it would be great if we could hang out again."

"Oh . . . kayyyyy." I sink onto the bench beside her and set my stuff down. "Tell me."

Gigi takes another breath. "Your obsession with the

curse grates on my nerves." She pauses. "It's all you ever talk about. You, your curse, your problems. And if it's not about the curse, then it's all about your art. You never wanted to talk about me or my interests."

I blink. What are her interests? And wondering makes me know she's right.

Gigi lays her hands in her lap. "I was excited when fifth grade ended, and thinking about us becoming middle schoolers, but you still wanted to do your color curses and talk about the llama loungers—"

"Lounge llamas," I correct.

"Yeah, whatever. Thing is, I'm over that stuff. I moved on. You never noticed. You haven't noticed a lot of things, like Hudson catching feelings for you—"

"What? No, we just both—"

"Or Curtis's crush on Bailee. I liked them both and you were clueless. I tried talking to you about it and other things, but you never wanted to talk about boys or crushes or basketball." It all comes rushing out of Gigi's mouth.

I press my lips together and listen.

"And I hated being squished in the middle on the bus. Plus, we only ever did what you wanted, like art club, when I don't even like to draw. Remember when I asked you to join the Lab Rats and you totally blew me off?"

"Wow." Recognition sinks down on me. It doesn't feel good, but I know it's all true, like how I've never gone to any of her clubs, and I didn't make Bailee's friends-forever wish. "You're right. I'm really sorry."

"I know you are." Gigi's voice comes out gentle. "I can see you're changing. You and Priscilla calling the truce, and you owning up to the cricket stuff to Priscilla was dope. No more lies, okay?"

"Deal." I stand in front of the mirror. The hair on the side of my head has frizzed from my shower. "Can I use this?" I pick up her brush.

"Of course."

I remove my ponytail holder and brush through my hair until it smooths.

"And please, no more lounging llama stuff." Gigi packs her PE clothing into a pocket of her backpack. "It was fun when we were younger, but . . ."

I blush, thinking about the new pajamas I love so much. "Thanks for the invitation on Friday. And for giving me another chance after I was such a lousy friend."

"Yep." She says this with a smile, the old smile she used to give me when we'd hang out.

My heart glows with brilliant beams of sunshine gold, but I keep the color to myself.

"I appreciate you telling me the truth." I weave the

270

ponytail holder back into my hair.

"So here's the deal. On Friday, a bunch of us girls will get ready together, and then the guys will come over—Hudson, Ryan, Steven, and Justin." She pauses and her smile grows bigger.

"You already invited Justin!"

"Yep. I told him you'd be there. I hoped you'd say yes. Anyhow, I invited a few other sixth- and seventh-grade girls and guys to come over, hang out, and have my mom's spaghetti. And since it'll be too many people to fit in my mom's car, we'll take the city bus to school when it's time for the dance."

"That sounds awesome!" I hand back her brush. I've missed Gigi so much. The smell of garlic cooking in her house. Her mom's big hugs. Her dad's deep laughter. But I think of Bailee. It wouldn't be fair if I ruin the fun for her. "What did Bailee say?"

"What do you mean?"

"She's super-mad at me about the crickets, so I don't know if she'll want to come to your house if I'm there." I take a breath and sigh it out. "It's her choice. If she doesn't want me there, I won't come."

"Ummm." Gigi loops her backpack straps on her shoulders. "Sage, I'm not inviting Bailee."

"What? Why not?"

"We're being honest still, right?"

My stomach tightens. "Um . . ."

Gigi goes on. "All that hand washing and the Clorox wipes and the germinator gig, and how we can never do things like photobooths because of how she freaks out about small spaces, and her screaming about bugs and—"

"Stop," I say. "Bailee is a lot more than that. She's generous and kind and honest and loyal."

Gigi shrugs. "Sage, we can like different people. You don't have to choose me or Bailee. I'm just saying I'm not inviting her. It's your call if you want to come or not, but you should." She smiles at me. "You can let me know later. I've got to run."

"No thanks." I don't need time to think about it. "If Bailee finds out she's the only one not invited, it'll make her feel awful. Count me out."

Gigi looks sad about my choice. "Okay."

I miss Bailee, and I decide right then that Miss Tammy's advice about using my own magic means I can fix my mess-up. I'm going to prove to Bailee that being best friends is stronger than any curse.

CHAPTER 33

I walk into the science classroom and face the graveyard of black-and-white solstice signs that litter the walls: "Solstice-sunset, tomorrow!" and "Winter Solstice Dance" and "24 hours until the solstice"—ominous reminders that time is running out. But I have to believe that with Priscilla and me teaming up, we're on the right track for lifting the curse for good. Our kindness plan will solidify it.

I sit at an open desk next to Steven. He's wearing a black T-shirt with a cloud and a lightning bolt.

"Any of that in our future?" I say, nodding to his shirt.

He touches the sides of his head. "Can't say for

sure. My mind is cloudy."

"Haha." I smile.

Class begins, and the teacher lectures on the life cycle of a plant. I doodle in my spiral notebook—unicorns, guinea pigs, and basketballs.

Basketballs?

Why would I draw basketballs?

I thumb through pages in my notebook, seeing the downhill regression of my sketches from last week to this week. Ugh. The curse-reverse is alive and strong. Maybe so strong that nothing can stop it now. Even wishing on a shooting star didn't help.

But I'm not giving up on my best friend. On the way to my next class, math, I spot Bailee and follow her down the hall. "Hey."

She doesn't look at me.

"I've decided no curse is going to ruin our friendship." I'm talking to her back, because she's rushing ahead of me. "I'm going to make this up to you."

"You're blaming the curse?" Bailee sounds annoyed.

"No! I'm saying our friendship is more than gold."

"Just go," she says.

I continue following her, rapid-firing everything Mrs. Rimmels said in the teachers' lounge and telling her how kindness may be the cure.

"Kindness?" Bailee says, fired up. "Are you trying

to guilt me into forgiving you?"

"No! I . . . I'm just trying to tell you what's up. I don't want to be a liar or have any more secrets. And I want you to know that I'm going to pay attention to things you're interested in, too. Like if there's a junior lawyers' club or something you want to join, I'll go with you, and—" We walk into math class.

Bailee stops at the doorway. "You know what would be kind? When I sit over here, you don't follow me."

My face flushes hot.

Bailee takes a seat at the far side of the room, and Curtis joins her.

Priscilla walks in, and I pull my shoulders back and focus my attention on what needs to be done in this moment. We nod like a handshake and then Priscilla and I exhaust ourselves trying to be kind to each other: "Pardon me." "No, pardon me." "Would you like this seat?" "No, please, you take the seat." "After you." "Please, you go first." It doesn't feel sincere, exactly, but we're really trying our best.

During the last fifteen minutes of class, Mrs. Floss writes three equations on the board. "Work the problems on your own, and when you're finished, you may use the last few minutes to talk through the solutions with a partner."

Bailee picks Curtis.

I say to Priscilla, "We've spent the last class, not to mention the whole morning, on nice things. Let's partner up and test the curse."

"Okay, how?"

"Solve the math problems and sketch three doodles."

"Smart," Priscilla says. "If the curse is over, my math will be perfect and your doodles will be perfect."

"Exactly."

Seven minutes later, we exchange papers and doodles. We check with Mrs. Floss to see whose math is right.

"Nice job, Sage," Mrs. Floss smiles at me. "All three are correct." She clears her throat. "And Priscilla, you got one right."

We return to our seats and compare doodles. Priscilla sketched a whole litter of puppies with cute noses, wagging tails, and floppy ears. I drew another lopsided basketball.

"Looks like my dad will never get out of jail." Priscilla's words come out choked.

The bell rings.

"Don't worry," I say, hearing the effort in my voice. "We'll figure out how to break the curse." Truth is, I'm scared we won't, and that even if my daddy does come home, I'll be moving to a new town with a sharp-edged momma.

Bailee straps her backpack to her shoulders, and just when I think she's going to walk out the door, she comes over to us. "I'm still mad at you," she says to me. "But since the clock is ticking, I'll help brainstorm ideas at lunch."

"Really?" A basketball-sized lump lodges in my throat. I want to hug her or thank her for giving me another chance, if that's what this is, but then Bailee turns to Priscilla. "I'm doing this for you. You helped me the other day when I needed to leave school after . . . the crickets."

"Thanks," Priscilla says. "I brought lunch from home, so I'll save seats." She gives us both a look of concern and starts to say something before she presses her lips together and heads off, leaving Bailee and me to walk to lunch in silence.

We pass more solstice signs, like countdown clocks stalking me.

In the cafeteria line, the smell of chicken stir-fry wafts toward us. I stay awkwardly silent, dying to talk to Bailee just like the good old days, but nervous that if I do, she'll walk away like she did in math. When it's our turn, we take chicken-and-rice bowls and small plates of carrot sticks. Across the room, Priscilla is already seated and talking with Jada, Gigi, and the guys.

Mrs. Downy lingers just a few steps away from the register, and I almost don't recognize her because she's wearing peach-colored lipstick, business-gray slacks, and a pressed white shirt.

When it's my turn to pay, I hand my lunch card to the cashier and then stand next to Mrs. Downy while I wait for Bailee. "You look nice, Mrs. Downy."

She either doesn't hear me or doesn't notice. Her eyes are laser focused on the people across the room, two men and a woman.

Bailee finishes paying and walks by like I don't exist, heading to the lunch table without me. It's like a kick in the gut. A painful lump grows in my throat and I stay next to Mrs. Downy, needing a moment to swallow down the hurt.

After a few moments, I say, "Who are those people?"

The strangers across the room are dressed in severe dark suits and carry clipboards and black pens. They walk to different spots in the cafeteria and mark notes on their papers. Mrs. Downy doesn't answer, her face in a worry knot.

One suited man has a mustache that twists up at the tips. The other man is tall and skinny and has curly brown hair. They follow behind a woman who is wearing dark-rimmed glasses. The three stop, look up, and glance from one light fixture to the next. They seem satisfied and check something off on their clipboards.

"That's right," Mrs. Downy says under her breath, "all bulbs working."

The woman hands the mustached man a white glove. He slips it on and runs his fingers over the windowsill and then across an empty tabletop. He inspects his glove and then sends a smile across the room to Mrs. Downy. She exhales and nods at him.

Mr. Lehman and Mrs. Rimmels, who usually eat in the teachers' lounge, walk up and join Mrs. Downy and me.

"Hello, Sage," Mrs. Rimmels says.

"What's going on?" I pick a carrot off my tray and crunch into it.

The suits walk to the silverware bin.

"Mrs. Downy is having her JOTY inspection and those are the judges," Mr. Lehman says.

The woman pulls on a pair of plastic gloves and picks up a fork by the gray metal stem. She twists it one way and then the other, adjusting her glasses as she peers at it closely.

"As you can see," says Mrs. Rimmels, "Mrs. Downy is a bit of a nervous wreck, even though we all know she is the best janitor statewide."

Mrs. Downy tries to smile, but her mouth barely quivers.

Mr. Lehman continues. "We are here to stand with Mrs. Downy in solidarity until the inspection is over."

"Thank you." Mrs. Downy wrings her hands. "What if they ask about Cricket-gate? I'm sure it happened because of that hole in the wall, but I don't want to blame the building committee."

"Don't fret." Mrs. Rimmels pats Mrs. Downy's arm. "You have done an immaculate job handling the mysterious outbreak. Answer honestly and let the chips fall where they may."

I cringe.

The inspector returns the fork to the bin and drops her plastic gloves in the garbage. The three judges check their clipboards.

I stand with my teachers and continue crunching carrots and watching the suits inspect our cafeteria. They squat and look under lunch tables. They check the outlet covers. They look at vents. They walk from corner to corner and then move toward Mrs. Downy.

She sucks in her breath.

I'm out of carrots. It's time for me to leave, but my legs are cement.

"Mrs. Downy," the woman says, "you already know James and Charles, but I have not formally introduced myself. I am Sarah Quigly, head of the JOTY committee. I'd like to personally tell you that your cafeteria is beautiful."

That's right. I smile and take a breath. The Ms. Quigly woman vibes a friendly fuchsia color even though she's wearing all black. I have a good feeling about her.

"Spick-and-span. A model of cleanliness."

"Thank you." Mrs. Downy's voice shakes.

"Your entire school is spotless," says the inspector with the mustache. The other two judges nod.

"The hallways, too," Ms. Quigly adds.

The cafeteria buzzes with conversation, movement, and laughter, and I stand there grinning.

"We are very lucky to have Mrs. Downy at Gold-view K–8," says Mrs. Rimmels. "She keeps our school sparkling."

Ms. Quigly smiles kindly and adjusts her glasses. "Now, Mrs. Downy, there are rumors about an alleged bug incident at your school. We'd like to give you an opportunity to go on the record and give your side of the story."

A clammy feeling spreads over my face and neck.

The other two judges click their black pens and hold them, ready to write.

"Well." Mrs. Downy clears her throat. "You won't find a single bug in this school. Everything has been taken care of."

"That's true!" I say.

"*Shhhh*," Mr. Lehman says softly.

The inspectors focus on Mrs. Downy. "You're saying there were bugs?" says the mustached man. "In your gym. In your school. Is that correct?"

"Yes," Mrs. Downy says solemnly. She looks down and stares at the man's shiny black shoes.

"Oh," he says softly. "Bugs are attracted to food crumbs and standing water, all of which fall under your charge."

"Yes, that's correct," Mrs. Downy says respectfully. "I have no explanation."

I squeeze my hands together. Words compete in my mind—*infamous to famous, infamous to famous*. If I confess, I'll be disqualified from the Noodler contest and everyone will keep thinking of me as Shady Sassafras. But if I don't tell, I'll be a fraud and there'll be no point in a kindness campaign, not if I'm going to let Mrs. Downy fail.

The mustached judge's mouth twists. Mrs. Quigly's face floods with regret. The skinny, curly-haired man reaches into his suit pocket and takes out three red pens. He quietly hands one to each inspector.

Infamous to famous.

Mrs. Rimmels pats Mrs. Downy's arm again.

My ears drum.

The judges uncap their red pens.

My shoulders feel like I'm carrying a Winnebago. "Um."

The pens move in slow motion toward the papers on the clipboards.

My throat tightens. I squeak out, "Excuse me?"

"Now is not a good time," Mr. Lehman says kindly.

"But I have a confession," I say. "The crickets were imported!"

Infamous.

The red pens stop moving.

"I . . . I am the one who brought crickets to school. They did not get in because of uncleanliness."

"Please explain," Ms. Quigly says.

"I purchased crickets from the pet store. I brought them to school. And I put them in another student's locker." I swallow. "As a prank."

The judges gasp.

"Young lady," the mustached man says, "do you realize—"

"We will deal with her, sir," Mr. Lehman says. "And I assure you, Mrs. Downy rid the school of Sage's prank swiftly and unequivocally, and there have been no crickets since."

I stare at the shoelaces of my new purple Converse.

"Well." Ms. Quigly turns to Mrs. Downy, her tone friendly. "This is a whole different set of circumstances."

The judges return the red pens to the curly-haired man, and he drops them into his pocket.

I exhale.

They continue talking to Mrs. Downy, but I don't hear what they say, because Mr. Lehman and Mrs. Rimmels pull me aside.

Mrs. Rimmels speaks softly. "You, my dear, have after-school detention for two weeks, where you will assist Mrs. Downy in whatever cleaning capacity she needs. You may start after the winter holiday break so you have an opportunity to let your mother know why you'll be coming home late."

"Does this mean I can't go to the dance?" I ask.

"No, the dance is part of our science program, so we still expect you to come." She winks at me.

Mr. Lehman's face droops sadder than I've ever seen it. "Sage, I'm so sorry you made a bad choice with the crickets, though I'm really proud of you for coming clean. Unfortunately, a detention disqualifies you from the Noodler contest."

And just like that, my big chance for changing the Sassafras name is over.

CHAPTER 34

Tears wet my face. Mr. Lehman holds my tray while Mrs. Rimmels hugs me. She pulls a Kleenex from her dress pocket and hands one over. "I'm proud of you for your honesty." She taps the "Be Kind" button on her collar.

I spend a few minutes blowing my nose before joining my friends. When I go to my lunch table, I take a breath. "Sorry, you guys." I clutch my tray and stare at the chicken-and-rice dish. "I . . . I did Cricket-gate. I brought the crickets to school, and it was mean and thoughtless, and I honestly feel terrible, and I'm really sorry." I sniffle. "If I could take it back I would. I already let Mrs. Downy know, and I'm officially disqualified from the Noodler contest, but there are plenty of great artists at this table, so I'm sure one of you can bring in a win for our school."

"Dang it," Hudson says.

I nod and look down, holding in more tears.

"Everyone knows you would've won. You're the best artist."

"Thanks, Hud." I put down my tray in a spot next to him and climb into the bench. "That's nice of you to say. Some days I'm the best, and some days it's you."

He makes protest noises.

"It's true," I say. Gigi's honesty made me realize that sometimes friends don't really see each other. "You know what else is true. If I had been honest with Bay, I would never have broken this rule. She wouldn't have let me."

Curtis laughs. "True that."

Bailee gives me a hesitant smile. "I'm not sure there's a no-bringing-bugs-to-school rule in our student handbook . . . but there should be."

I laugh, relieved she said something. Baby steps.

"You should've waited until after the Noodler contest to confess about Cricket-gate," Ryan says.

"No, I couldn't let Mrs. Downy take the fall. It was lousy enough that I did it to Priscilla and Bailee and everyone."

"We called a truce, remember," Priscilla says. "And like I already said, I forgive you about the crickets, Sage. I think we all do."

My friends around the table nod—I look to Bailee, and though she doesn't agree, she doesn't look away. Her brown eyes glint with a spark of gold. Hudson smiles at me; so do Steven, Curtis, Jada, Ryan, Gigi, and Justin. I pause. When did Justin arrive? My heart flutters. "H-hi." My voice wobbles.

"Hey." He gives me that awesome lopsided grin.

A smile spreads across my face, and all the friendship and forgiveness at the table gives me an idea.

"What do you guys think of calling today and every solstice eve Goldview Kindness Day?"

"What does that mean?" Hudson asks.

"It means be a friend. Like how Priscilla and I became friends. And like how Curtis and Justin forgave me for being a big jerk this week. And you, Hudson, calling me the best artist, because you were trying to make me feel better."

Hudson grins. "And because it's true. Sometimes."

I smile back. "I'm thinking for Kindness Day everyone can find ways to be generous or sympathetic or thoughtful or nice." I turn to Gigi. "And honest, like you, Gigi."

She shrinks.

"Seriously," I say. "It was kind that you told me the truth about how you feel. It doesn't mean I agree with everything you said, because I like calling myself a lounge llama and saying my color exclamations. But you told me in a nice way." I shrug. "I don't know, now that you let out the truth, it feels like we can be real with each other." I fiddle with the end of my hair, feeling a twinge of awkwardness. "Um, so what do you guys think about Kindness Day?"

"It's a great idea!" Priscilla says. "I second the motion. Let's make today, solstice eve, Goldview Kindness Day."

Priscilla and I exchange looks, and I know she's finally on board with me believing that the community fed the curse and helped keep it alive. Now we're relying on our friends and neighbors to help us end it for good.

"I third the motion," Bailee says, and offers me some of her pomegranate hand gel. The special kind. I bust out my biggest smile of the week.

"You forgive me?" I say.

And she says, "Duh."

Classes go well, teachers are happy, and we accomplish a pretty awesome day of practicing kindness—Hudson scoots a spider out the window, Bailee picks up trash, and Priscilla and I continue falling all over each other trying to be helpful. Five minutes before the last bell of the day, I say to Priscilla, "Let's have a doodle-off and test if Kindness Day was enough to squash the curse."

Before we can try, the school loudspeaker pipes into our history classroom.

"Hello," the secretary says. "We need Priscilla Petty to come down to the office."

Priscilla's shoulders visibly tense. Mine do, too.

"It's going to be all right," Priscilla says shakily as she gathers up her stuff.

"Yep," I say.

The door clicks shut behind her.

"I hope everything is okay with her dad," I whisper to Bailee.

"It has to be." Bailee crosses her fingers. I cross my toes.

The bell rings, and Bay and I drop off our books in our lockers. Everyone is buzzing about the dance and the long holiday break, happy that none of the teachers gave us homework. We clang our locker doors shut, click the locks in place, and head outside into the cool pine air.

"Hey, Bailee! Sage!" Gigi runs up the sidewalk to catch us. Her voice is breathy. "I'm wondering if you guys would like to come over tomorrow for my mom's spaghetti and marinara and to get ready for the dance. A bunch of people are coming."

Phew! Bailee never has to know Gigi invited me without her.

Instead of smiling, Bailee shakes her head fast and says, "No." She watches her feet as we walk to the bus. "It's okay, Gigi. Part of being kind means you have to be honest, and I've already heard from enough people that I'm too much of a germaphobe for you."

"Listen to me," Gigi says. "I'm sorry. Sure, I don't like the germaphobe stuff, but I was dumb to blow off our friendship because of it."

Bailee stays quiet.

"I miss you. I want you to come over, and to prove it, I have some rules." Gigi says "rules" in a playful tone.

Bailee looks up. "Okay, now you're speaking my language."

"Rule one, you're not allowed to force everyone to use hand gel." Gigi smiles. "Rule two, I'll promise you that my parents will wash their hands before they cook, they always do, so you're not allowed to push gel on them, either. Three, if you want to use hand gel, I won't judge you. I really do want you to come. Please say yes."

"You had me at 'rules,'" Bailee says.

I laugh, loud and goofy. We line up at the bus stop, rubbing warmth into our arms, the air chillier than it has been all week. I'm so confident the curse is lifting that I'm going to beg Mr. Melvin to drive extra fast so I can race home and see if Momma is back to normal.

I look across the parking lot, trying to find Priscilla's car. But Priscilla steps in line with us at the bus stop. "Hey?"

Priscilla's shoulders sag. "Goldview Kindness Day didn't work."

"What? No. How do you know?"

"My mother called the office to let them know I'd need to take the bus home."

"That's good," I say. "You said you liked riding the bus."

"I do," Priscilla says. "But the reason I'm taking it home is because she forgot to charge the car. That's not like my mother at all."

As she says this, we hear a car in the parking lot honk and honk and *hooooooooonk!*

Bailee, Priscilla, Gigi, and I look over.

It's my mom. And she's driving a new car!

CHAPTER 35

You'd think riding home on fancy tan leather seats with new-car smell would be super-fun, but Momma's mood is worse than ever. Her frown lines etch deep in her face, and she won't give any of my friends a ride home.

The second I buckle my seat belt, she complains about her day—phone calls with accountants and lawyers, and everyone wanting something from her. The slow-crawling pick-up line adds to her frustration. "Geez, what's going on?" Momma leans left and tries to see around the Jeep in front of us.

"This is how the car line always moves after school," I say. Poor Momma looks so tired, and I'm about to thank her for picking me up, until she hollers at the car in front of us, "Hurry up!" She jams her hand on the horn. *Hooooooonk!*

Heads turn our way. "Momma! People have to drive slowly in a school parking lot."

"Please don't manage me, Sage. I'm not in the mood."

Her words feel like a slap, and I'm inching low in my seat when a Mimi Glosser song comes on the radio. I reach to turn it up. This will change her mood.

Momma immediately clicks it off and says, "My head hurts." She sighs and forces a kinder tone. "Sorry, I'm exhausted from all the packing."

I look back at my bus, full of my friends laughing and smiling.

We finally pull out of the lot, and Momma speeds down the road. A few minutes later, the headache must ease, because she clicks on the radio. Instead of playing fun music, she selects a channel where a newscaster says, "With only a few leaves remaining in Goldview, I can safely say that fall is behind us, and just in time for the winter solstice."

Kindness Day was a bust, but maybe Priscilla's wish will come true and we'll magically have a thundersnow and pink lightning. I squeeze my hands in prayer.

"Clear skies in the forecast," the newscaster says.

I slump lower in my seat. Just like I thought, Priscilla wished on a Saturday and probably deactivated the candle. I'm out of ideas. And tomorrow is the deadline for a whole generation. I might be doomed to be cursed for the rest of my life!

We zoom past the pet store, and I imagine all the dogs, reptiles, crickets, and guinea pigs in their cages, living their lives without a worry.

Guinea pigs?

My brain kicks into gear. That's it! Suddenly I know what needs to be done to lift the curse. I've been focused on getting help from the community, but I've forgotten to involve the two most important people.

Momma drives on Seventh Street and we pass Minerva's. The "Closed" sign still looms on the door. But now I have hope. A few minutes later, Momma parks at our apartment complex, and I race upstairs to call Priscilla. *Miss Tammy said people can make their own magic*, I think, squeezing the phone. That's exactly what we need to do. After three rings, Priscilla answers. I can hear my friends on the bus laughing and having a good time. "Hey," I say. "I've got it."

"What? The plague? What are we talking about?" Priscilla laughs, but this time it's not mean. It's a laugh that says we're becoming friends.

"No, I've got a solution. The curse didn't start with the pink lightning," I say. "It started when the boa constrictor ate my momma's guinea pig!"

"I'm listening," Priscilla says.

"Have Bailee scoot close so you both can hear at the same time."

A moment later, Bailee says, "I'm here."

I share my plan.

"I think this just might work," Priscilla says.

"I sure hope so," Bailee adds.

It better. The idea is our final shot.

CHAPTER 36
FRIDAY, DECEMBER 21

On Friday, I convince Momma to drive by Minerva's before dropping me off at Gigi's to hang out before the dance. The shop is still closed. I'm not surprised.

Gigi's family lives in a small white house with a neat yard and a topaz-blue door. When the door swings open, I breathe in the familiar scents of her house: roasting tomatoes, yeasty bread, and sizzling garlic.

"Sage!" Gigi's mom hugs me at the front door. I hold on to her a moment too long, and she laughs when I don't let go. "It's good to see you, too, sweetie."

Her papa hugs me, too. "We've missed you around

here." His Italian accent is strong and joyful.

"Thank you for having all of us over."

"You know we love a big party. Another excuse for Martina's cooking." He pats his round belly and laughs as Gigi's mother beams.

In the living room, the couches and end tables have been pushed aside and a long row of card tables stretches the full length of the room. White paper napkins and mason jar water glasses sit at each spot.

"Come on," Gigi says. "We're getting ready back here."

I follow Gigi to her room. Music is playing from Priscilla's phone. Bailee sits in a white chair, and Priscilla stands behind her, French braiding her hair. Jada is trying on an Egyptian-blue shirt and twisting in the mirror to see herself at different angles.

"That looks cute on you, Jada." I set my backpack on the floor and sit on Gigi's starburst quilt bedding. "I love your hair, Bay. You guys all look great."

"Thanks," Bailee and Jada say.

"Why'd you bring your backpack?" Gigi asks.

"I have a group project I'm going to announce when everyone arrives."

"I've missed that about you," Gigi says, beaming. "Your fun ideas."

"Can't wait," Priscilla says. "By the way, you look

great. I thought you were going to get ready here with us."

"My momma wouldn't let me leave without forcing me to dress how she wanted, and then she insisted on fixing my hair, too." I'm wearing a blue jean skirt with a soft, snowball-white sweater, and instead of a ponytail, my hair is in smooth waves.

"Sounds familiar," Priscilla says, giving me a secret look.

"Your mom has good taste," Jada says. "You look super-pretty."

"Yeah," Gigi agrees.

"Thanks. You guys do, too."

"Does anyone want lemonade?" Gigi asks. "My dad made it with San Pellegrino, so it's bubbly."

We all say yes.

"I'll help you," Jada says, following her out of the room.

The door clicks shut behind them, leaving me, Priscilla, and Bailee alone.

"I tried to swing by Minerva's," I say.

"Me too," Bailee says. "Still closed."

"How are you holding up, Priscilla?"

Priscilla secures the end of Bailee's braid with a black silk hair tie, her face serious. "Stressed for my dad. He's out on bail again. Your plan has to work."

"It will." I wish I could sound more certain. "Did your mom agree to pick us up from here?"

"Yep," Priscilla says. "She's really excited to see all our outfits."

Bailee scrapes her chair around to face me and asks, "Everything in place on your end?"

"Well." I fidget with the key on my necklace. "Not everything."

"Oh, geez. What happened?"

"I couldn't convince Momma to be a chaperone, but Miss Tammy was at our apartment watching her fix my hair, and when Momma said no for the umpteenth time, Miss Tammy said she'd chaperone."

"And?" Priscilla's voice goes high.

"I told my momma she should drive Miss Tammy to drop her off at the school so she won't have to take the bus. Momma agreed. Now we just need to have your mom come to the parking lot at that same time and hope nothing goes wrong."

"Hope and pray," Priscilla says.

Gigi comes back with the lemonades, and we take our drinks to the front of the house as a bunch of kids arrive—first Curtis and Hudson. Next, Janet, Lily, and Shanie—Gigi's BFFs from science club. The doorbell rings again and in walks Steven. He's wearing a blue T-shirt that says, "I'm cirrus about weather." A few more classmates follow him through the door, including Ryan and a couple of seventh graders, and then Justin.

My stomach knots up. I take a step to the back of the gathering. Does my skirt fit okay? I smooth it down and notice my hands, wishing I had fixed my nail polish. I watch as Justin meets Gigi's parents and thanks them for inviting him over. The second he finishes shaking Gigi's papa's hand, he looks around the room . . .

. . . until he spots me! His eyes light up and he walks straight to me.

"Hi," I say. I cross my arms and then uncross them and wonder how my hair looks.

"Hey. You look great!"

I smile. "You do, too." He's wearing dark-wash jeans, a cobalt-blue shirt, a leather watch, and maybe cologne, because he smells like woodsy mountain air.

"I've never seen your hair down," he says. "It's pretty."

I smile at the ground.

"Oh, and Peaches wanted me to tell you hello." Justin gives me his awesome lopsided grin, and that fizzy apricot color I feel around him twirls across my collarbones.

I put on a jokey formal tone and say, "Please give Peaches my regards."

Justin laughs. "Will do."

Gigi clinks her lemonade glass with a silver fork. "Everyone, please come into the living room."

We gather at the card tables, the plates full of spaghetti. Steamy garlic bread and dipping bowls full of spiced olive oil sit in the center. I grab my backpack from Gigi's room and scoot it under my chair so I'm ready. I sit next to Bailee and Gigi, and Justin sits across from me. We eat and talk and laugh.

Priscilla says, "All right, Flores Phenom. Give us your forecast, and make it good." She's trying to sound lighthearted, but I know she's still hoping for pink lightning in case my plan doesn't do the trick.

The room quiets.

Steven looks out the big living room window and up at the sky. He stretches out his arm and then brings his microphone-thumb under his lips. "This is the Flores Phenom, reporting to you live from Gigi's Trattoria."

Gigi smiles. Her papa gives a big belly laugh.

"Current weather conditions: muggy with a chance of rain or snow."

"Okay! That's good," I say.

Gigi's science club friends give me an odd look.

"He's making it up as he goes, right?" Shanie says. "I didn't bring a coat or an umbrella."

"We're staying hopeful," Priscilla says, winking at me.

The food is delicious. I use the thick, crusty bread to sop up the garlic-and-basil marinara sauce. When my plate is clean, I clink my water glass with a fork, just like Gigi had earlier. "Attention! Attention, people."

I have to do this a few times before the room hushes. I stand up and set my backpack on my chair.

Gigi claps her hands. "Time for Sage's special project announcement!"

"That's right," I say. "As you all know, I'm personally not allowed to compete in the Noodler contest; however, I thought it would be fun if we created a group project."

I unzip my backpack and take out the notecard I've written on. "I've been thinking that family can mean more than just family at home. And since Mrs. Rimmels encourages us to look up words, I looked up the exact meaning of 'family' in the dictionary. Here's what it says." I look down at my notecard. "'Family is a social unit consisting of one or more adults together with the children they care for.'"

I reach into my backpack and remove my sketch of the school bus, the one I drew before my doodling abilities disappeared. "So far, I have Mr. Melvin in the driver's seat and me and Bailee nine rows down on the right."

"Ohhhh," Jada says.

I nod at her. "We are a family." I look from one friend to the next. "And I think it would be fun if everyone adds something to this sketch and we let Hudson finish it off—that is if you don't mind, Hudson."

He bangs his fist on the table and the silverware clatters. "I'd love to!"

It's not going to break the curse, but like Gigi said, everything can't be about me and my curse.

CHAPTER 37

At 3:30 p.m., Priscilla, Bailee, Justin, and I walk out of Gigi's house into the first day of winter. The other kids have already caught a ride on the city bus.

"Shortest day of the year," Bailee whispers to me. "We have an hour and nineteen minutes until sunset."

Justin glances at his watch and gives me an odd look.

I crack my knuckles. "Thanks." The cool air reaches through my sweater and brushes my skin. I look to both ends of the street. Mrs. Petty is late, and my insides twist with worry that we won't finish everything we need to do and make it to school by sundown.

Fifteen minutes later, Mrs. Petty finally pulls up the drive.

Priscilla takes the front seat, and Bailee, Justin, and I climb into the back. I've never been inside a car like this, with dozens of buttons and gadgets and a big computer screen on the dashboard. I scoot to the middle spot, and my leg touches Justin's, sending a flutter to my heart.

"Hi, kids," Mrs. Petty says.

"I love your car!" Justin says.

"Thanks for driving us." I buckle my seat belt.

"You're welcome." Mrs. Petty presses a button to close the moonroof. "It's getting chilly outside."

I nudge Bailee, giving her the cue. Even though we're behind schedule, we need Mrs. Petty to stay in the driveway until we convince her to make a stop.

"Oh," Bailee says. "I forgot something in Gigi's house. Would you mind waiting just a minute?"

"No problem," Mrs. Petty says in a friendly tone. Friendly like my momma used to be. Her blond hair is in a high ponytail and she seems relaxed, instead of in her usual uptight knot.

"You look nice, Mrs. Petty," I say.

"Thank you." She looks at her reflection in the rearview mirror and runs a hand over her cheek. "Seems I forgot my makeup today, but who has time for all that fuss?" She laughs. "Lately, I've been focused on more important things." She rubs Priscilla's back.

Priscilla looks at me in the rearview mirror, and I nod the go-ahead.

"Guess what, Mom?" Priscilla says, sort of loud and stiff. "Sage and I started a new school holiday."

"More than a school holiday," I say. "We're going to petition for a city holiday."

Justin glances between us. "Oh, right. Goldview Kindness Day. That's dope."

"That sounds sweet," Mrs. Petty says. "How did you two come up with that?"

"Um," I say, "well, as you must know, middle school can be a tough place, so we thought every solstice we should take a moment and build community through kindness."

"Solstice eve, right?" Justin says.

"No," Priscilla says nervously. "Goldview Kindness Day is actually today, on the solstice."

Justin scrunches his eyebrows, and I give him a just-go-with-it look.

"What a lovely idea!" Mrs. Petty says. "What are you—"

I interrupt. "Was middle school tough for you, Mrs. Petty?" My voice comes out squeaky.

Mrs. Petty pauses on my question. A honey-golden

leaf floats down to the car windshield. Maybe the last leaf of fall, the trees now bare. The sun inches lower, and my insides twist tighter. The clock on the dashboard reads 3:47.

"Some parts were good and some parts were difficult." She stares at me in the rearview mirror. "I'm sure you know all about me and your mother."

I nod. "I'll bet you both wish you did things differently. I know my momma does."

Now it's her turn to nod. She clicks on the windshield wipers and swishes the leaf away.

I clear my throat, giving Priscilla the cue to take this to the next level. Justin stays quiet, smart enough to notice something is going down. It makes me like him even more.

"Um, so what would you have done if you had a kindness day in middle school, Mom?" Priscilla sounds awkward.

"Well, I probably would've found a way to be helpful, or maybe I would have sat with someone who was eating alone, or—"

"Do you have anything specific you might have done?" I ask, wanting to speed this up. "You know, with my momma?"

She looks in the mirror again like she's trying to figure out what I'm up to.

"I know my momma feels bad about all the Contrarium stuff. She wishes she never fixed herself up for the barn dance. To this day she feels terrible about your poison oak outbreak."

"She told you that?"

"Mmmhmm," I say with crossed fingers. "And I'll bet there are things you wish you could undo."

"Well, sure."

"Like what?" Priscilla and I say at the same time.

"You two sure are curious."

"Like what, Momma . . . um, Mom," Priscilla says.

"Well, certainly the snake incident."

"Right!" I say a bit too brightly.

"What is the snake incident?" Justin says.

Mrs. Petty explains how her boa constrictor ate Momma's guinea pig pup.

Bailee steps out of Gigi's front door and adjusts her glasses. I give her a head shake, and she goes back inside the house.

"Here's an idea." My voice squeaks, making me wish I had some of Jada's acting talent so I could sound like I had just thought of this. "You could always buy her a new guinea pig."

"Yeah!" Priscilla says.

Justin looks like he's trying to solve a puzzle. I realize I am still sitting right beside him even though there's room for me to scoot over. I smile at him.

Mrs. Petty laughs. "A grown woman doesn't just buy another woman a guinea pig. Your mother would think I'm nuts."

I lean forward and grab the back of her seat. "My momma would love it."

"She would?" Mrs. Petty stops laughing.

"Mm-hmm." I nod fast. "It'd be a huge gesture. More than you think."

Justin says, "We have three guinea pig pups in the store right now."

I could hug him.

"Oh, Mom, please say yes!" Priscilla says.

"Are you asking me to do this right now? Today, on the way to the dance?"

"Yes!" we say.

"It might be better if I just pick one up tomorrow and deliver it over the weekend."

"Tomorrow is too late!" Priscilla and I say at the same time.

Mrs. Petty gives each of us an odd look.

"Um," I add, "you could do it for Kindness Day."

"Well, if you think it would be okay," she says slowly. "I've always felt tremendously guilty about all that."

She has? Even before the curse reversed? I wonder.

"I know, Mom," Priscilla says hopefully, and picks up her mother's hand. She holds it, and there are tears in Priscilla's eyes, because she knows if the curse lifts, there's no guarantee her mom will be this kind moving forward.

The door opens, and Bailee climbs into the car. "All set?"

"Yep." My plan is in action. I hope we make it before sunset.

CHAPTER 38

The guinea pig pup is adorable—little triangle ears, a button nose, and sweet brown eyes. It's soft and cute and loveable. We take turns holding it, and it's Bailee's turn now. I lean over to scratch its head.

Where is Momma? I wonder. Sunset is at 4:39 p.m. and it's already 4:30. My stomach twists with loop-the-loops. The sun is slowly dipping behind the mountains.

The school parking lot is covered in freshly fallen leaves, and we wait in the car because the weather has turned too cold to stand outside. What's taking her so long?

Mrs. Petty shifts in the front seat, darting looks around. "Are you sure your mother will like this?"

"I'm one hundred percent positive." I lift the pup from Bailee's lap and hand it to Mrs. Petty. "Here, it's your turn again."

Petting it calms her.

Bright blue balloons hang from the school entrance and flutter when the breeze comes and goes.

I look left and right out each window, the sky still mostly clear.

"Are you sure she's coming?" Priscilla says, her voice shaking. "Maybe we should drive to your apartment?"

"She'll be here. She's driving Miss Tammy."

Minutes go by. The sun dips lower. The pup makes a chittering noise, and I nervous-laugh and pet its adorable red-brown head.

Knock, knock! It's Miss Tammy tapping on the window. "Hey, what are you guys doing out here? Isn't the party inside?"

I fling open the door and my friends follow me out of the car. "Miss Tammy?"

"Hey, Spice." Miss Tammy hugs her coat to her body and few drops of rain dot her face. She poofs open a tiny preschooler-sized umbrella decorated with little yellow ducks.

"Don't laugh," she says. "I borrowed this from the café."

"Where's—"

The rain picks up. "Oh, goodness," Miss Tammy says. "Come huddle with me, you guys."

We move closer to her tiny umbrella while I search the parking lot for Momma's new car. The umbrella is no help and rain still dots our heads and backs. "Where did Momma park?"

"She didn't."

The engine from the city bus grumbles across the street. The sun is halfway down.

"Oh no. You took the bus here?"

"Sure did. It was raining much harder on our end of town, and your momma couldn't figure out how to turn on the windshield wipers in that fancy new car of hers."

Priscilla's blue eyes flood with worry. My heart drops. "What time is it, Justin?"

He looks at his watch. "Four thirty-five." Justin reads my face. "Is everything okay?"

Bailee shakes her head. Only four minutes left!

Mrs. Petty climbs out of the car, cradling the guinea pig against her chest. She joins our huddle. "This weather." She looks to the clouds. "You all should hurry inside."

More drips patter down and then a few white snow-flakes fall and stick to the pup's little brown body.

My heart aches. This was our last chance. Mine and Priscilla's. To get our mommas in the same place at the same time. To end the curse. To save the next genera-tion. To fix the Sassafras name. To help our daddies. To fix everything.

"It's four thirty-six," Bailee says.

I grab Priscilla's hand. "I'm sorry." The rain and snow fall harder and wet our backs, and the sun droops another inch. Our time is about up. Even if we raced across town at top speed, we'd never make it to my apartment before sunset. I squeeze Priscilla's hand. "I'm sorry I couldn't get my momma here."

"You did everything you could," she says.

The city bus rumbles away and up walks Momma. "Momma!"

"I didn't say she didn't come," Miss Tammy says. "I just said she couldn't figure out her car."

Momma's eyes meet mine, and I leave our huddle and throw myself at her in a hug.

She laughs, her face dripping with rain. "This dance seemed important to you, Sage. Tammy reminded me you're growing up and you may not give me many more invitations to chaperone, so I didn't want to miss seeing you enjoy this solstice."

My heart fills with helium.

Suddenly, Momma startles. "Oh!" She clears her throat and turns stiff and formal, facing Mrs. Petty. "Hello, Candice."

Priscilla places her arm around her mother's waist and gently pulls her closer to Momma and me, softly saying, "Go ahead, Mom."

Mrs. Petty stares down at the pup in her hands. With a shaky voice she says, "Hi, Rosemary. I . . . I'm . . . sorry." Her voice chokes, but she takes a breath, lifts her downcast eyes, and says, "I'm truly sorry for years of unkind remarks, sarcasm, and hurtful gossip. I'm sorry for jealousy and stupid competition. And mostly, I'm sorry I lost you as a friend." She holds out the guinea pig pup. "Please forgive me."

Momma is statue-still. She doesn't say anything. I loop my arm in hers and whisper the same words as Priscilla, "Go ahead, Momma."

Clouds, rain, snow, and the final golden ray of sunlight hover over us.

Momma reaches forward, cupping her hands. Mrs. Petty passes the little pup to her, and when Momma and Mrs. Petty's hands touch, their eyes meet, and they both smile. Momma draws the pup to her chest and kisses the top of its head. "Hello, Cinnamon."

A snowflake lands on Cinnamon's tiny nose, and

it's so cute that Priscilla, Mrs. Petty, Momma, and I laugh and hug and we're in a circle when the sky pops and turns watermelon pink and down comes a flash of pink lightning. It hits the ground between us, and a powerful zap travels up my legs and zings through my fingertips. The four of us are still touching, hand to hand, hand to shoulder, arms linked. None of us let go until we know we all felt the same thing. And the sun disappears behind the mountains.

CHAPTER 39

Anyone interested in knowing it's now four forty
p.m.?" Justin says, rain dripping off his hair.
"Or going for a swim?"

We burst out laughing and crying, not from the
zap or from fear, but from knowing we are going
to be all right. I exchange a look with Momma and
then with Priscilla. Momma's and Mrs. Petty's eyes
meet and there's more than a truce there: there's the
promise of forgiveness and a rekindled friendship.
They smile and laugh again, and I know the curse is
behind us.

"Are you guys okay?" Bailee asks.

"Yes," I say.

Momma hands Bailee the pup and squeezes my hands. "Are you really okay, honey? Are you injured anywhere?" Mrs. Petty fusses over Priscilla, too.

"I'm good," I say.

"You're not just saying that?" Momma cups my face in her hands and leans forward so we're nose to nose. "I'm here for you, Sage."

"I know you are."

"No. I'm really here for you. And I'm going to do a better job of taking care of things—food on the table, gas in the car, all that."

I nod.

"I know you don't like to talk to me about what's going on in your life, but I'm willing to do whatever it takes to win your trust."

I drop my gaze, but Momma lifts my chin. She sees my unspoken words, so I say them out loud. "That means you can't always freak out, and you have to stop ignoring the hard stuff."

"Deal," she says. "I give you my word." She pulls me in for a tight hug, and tears join the rain on my face.

"Come along, everyone," Miss Tammy says.

We hurry inside to the school, soaked to the bone. Rain and snow plaster my hair to my face, and my sweater drips a trail of water.

"Well, hello." Mr. Melvin swings open the school door, greeting our sopping-wet crew. He's dressed from head to toe in the nicest blue suit I've ever seen. "Come in, come in. You all must be freezing."

Momma, Miss Tammy, Mrs. Petty, Priscilla, Bailee, Justin, and I drip a puddle right in the center of the school lobby. A Mimi Glosser song is playing in the distance. Miss Tammy shivers and struggles to remove her wet coat.

"Let me help you with that," Mr. Melvin says.

"Thank you," Miss Tammy says, her eyes bright.

He takes her soaked coat and wraps his dry one around her. "Here you go. I wish I had more coats to share." He spies Cinnamon in Bailee's arms. "May I?"

Bailee hands the pup to Mr. Melvin, and he dries Cinnamon with his nice white shirt sleeve.

I shiver.

"Goodness me," Mrs. Rimmels says, coming around the corner. "There must have been a lightning strike. The power went out for a full minute, but we have the dance under control now."

I gasp—decked out in cornflower-blue cowboy boots and walking right beside my favorite teacher, is . . .

Minerva!

"This is absotively the best!" Minerva says to me

and my friends. "I'm so delighted to see you all here!"

"Blue bunny rabbits!" I screech. "You?"

Mrs. Rimmels and Minerva are both dressed in sweaters decorated in a snowflake pattern, long flowy skirts, and matching boots.

Priscilla and Bailee gawk as hard as I do.

"Oh!" Mrs. Rimmels says. "You've met my niece?" She turns to Minerva. "You know my students? What a surprise."

Mrs. Rimmels could use some acting lessons from Jada.

Momma, Mrs. Petty, and Justin shiver.

"We can't stand here chatting when you lot are soaked to the skin," Mrs. Rimmels says. "Follow me. All of you. I'll let you borrow clothing from the office bin."

Priscilla, Bailee, and I bust out laughing.

CHAPTER 40

On the drive to the court building in Denver to hear Daddy's appeal, I write down the rest of the story:

There were enough outfits in the ugly bin that me, Momma, Miss Tammy, Mrs. Petty, Priscilla, Bailee, and Justin were able to find something dry to wear. We wore the borrowed outfits to the dance, and guess what, no matter how ugly our clothing was, or how much my hair frizzed, we had fun and Justin still looked cute. He's a really great dancer, too.

Mrs. Rimmels claimed her niece, Minerva, had moved here from Vermont. My lie detector went off, but that's the story Mrs. Rimmels is giving, and she's sticking to it.

Mr. Petty's accountants discovered hackers were siphoning off money and making it look like Mr. Petty was embezzling, so he returned to work at the bank. Mrs. Downy, as anyone could have guessed, won her fifth JOTY plaque. Miss Tammy and Mr. Melvin struck up a romance. I'll bet that would have happened sooner had he visited Goldview Café for his morning coffee instead of Java Hut. I'm happy to report their romance is still going strong. Momma and Mrs. Petty aren't perfect. They have their nice days and their bossy-mom days. I think most mothers do. Momma and I talk more. And Momma is doing a better job listening rather than overreacting or pretending things away. I'm doing a better job trusting her.

We're using the money from Re-Bay to buy a house in our old neighborhood. It's close to Bailee's house and close enough for Justin to ride his bike over, too. Priscilla, Jada, Gigi, Bailee, and I all hang out now. It makes me think that maybe the gold of old seasons doesn't stay, but change can have its bright colors, too.

And Doodle for Noodler—our group project won! Hudson earned the scholarship since he completed the project, and Noodler gave all of us tickets to the Mimi Glosser concert, where they interviewed our group on national television! Hudson talked about the art, Steven gave a Flores Report, and I spoke about Goldview

Kindness Day and how we plan to celebrate it every winter solstice. I'm trying to make it a national holiday. I might even write a book about the true story of how it came about. Oh, and by the way, I became a tiny bit famous for about one minute. I'm still a little bit infamous, too, but I've given up trying to manage what people think about me.

I finish writing this as Momma parks the car. We walk up the marble courthouse steps, hand in hand. When we step inside the courtroom, I meet Daddy's eyes and I make sure to smile so he knows I'm working on forgiving him.

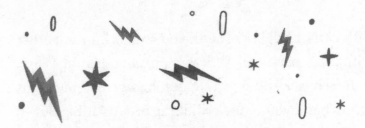

ACKNOWLEDGMENTS

Thank you to my generous and genius agent, Jennifer Rofé, of the Andrea Brown Literary Agency, and her wonderful assistant, Kayla Cichello, for helping me in so many ways, including brainstorming the magic. To my always-brilliant editor, Maria Barbo, you are a star and a delight to work with. To assistant editor Stephanie Guerdan, thank you for your astute catches and *Star Wars* expertise. To Anna-Maria Crum and Hilari Bell for much-needed help, encouragement, and early plot planning. Special thanks to Tammy Parsons: you were instrumental in so many ways. Thank you for not only being one of my best friends since middle school, but also for reading several drafts and fielding one hundred texts where I bombarded you with questions about this story, and to Brian Parsons for "Curtis's" jokes! To Steven Mooser and Lin Oliver for starting the SCBWI. To Jerilyn Patterson, John Christenson, and Penny Berman for dropping everything to provide me with early feedback. Thank you so much to my other critiquing partners, Will Limón, and Elaine Pease: your feedback and smart suggestions were tremendous help! Thank you to my critiquing groups at Big Sur in the Rockies, including my newest critiquing partner, Sylvia Liu! Thank you to Jenny Wixson for your help with Spanish and for guiding me in creating Steven Flores, a third-generation character from Honduras. Thank you to Stephanie Wilburn from Body & Soul Salon & Day Spa for helping me understand my character Jada. To the RMC-SCBWI illustrator community, Kaz Windness, Dow Phumiruk, Julie Rowan-Zoch, and Anna-Maria Crum, for helping me understand art terms. To Kelli Narans for insight on the law, and to readers for stretching their imagination when I took liberties with the law. To Celia Sinoway for lakeside chats, and to Karen Churnside for garden-fresh soup. To Jason Hussong, for fueling me with peanut M&M's. To the Nagy sisters, and to Sydney Stanton's book club. To the Berberians, Marlo, Renée, and Paul, for brainstorming "pranks," and to Sally Spear, Lauren Sabel, Denise Vega, and Brian Papa for listening to me talk through story problems. To Noelle and Cayman, because I love you. And to Steve Tomsic for your support and insightful edits, and for convincing me to swap the mouse for a guinea pig pup.

MORE MAGICAL MAYHEM AWAITS IN KIM TOMSIC'S FIRST BOOK:

Megan Meyers has a foolproof plan to reinvent herself at her new school. Good-bye, dorky math nerd; hello, friend magnet! But her first day is weird to the tenth power. When she's dared to "make something exciting happen," Megan is thrown into the middle of an epic popular-girl power struggle. So, with nothing to lose as her classroom's cat clock chimes 11:11, she makes a wish. But wishes come with unexpected side effects, and soon Megan finds herself making bigger and bigger promises to her new friends. And as her problems grow exponentially worse, Megan begins to wonder if magic was really the purrfect key to her fresh start after all.